CHRISTMAS MALE

BY
CARA SUMMERS

First published in Great Britain 2010
Harlequin Mills & Boon Limited,
Eton House, 18-24 Paradise Road, Richmond, Surrey TW9 1SR

© Carolyn Hanlon 2009

ISBN: 978 0 263 88152 3

14-1210

Harlequin Mills & Boon policy is to use papers that are natural, renewable and recyclable products and made from wood grown in sustainable forests. The logging and manufacturing processes conform to the legal environmental regulations of the country of origin.

Printed and bound in Spain
by Litografia Rosés S.A., Barcelona

RITA® Award nominee *Cara Summers* is currently working on her thirty-fifth story, a new Blaze® romance. Her books have won several awards, including two Golden Leaves, three Golden Quills, an Award of Excellence, a Holt Medallion and a Lifetime Achievement Award from *RT Book Reviews*. Who does she credit with inspiring her to become a romance writer? Her dad, who was always an avid reader of genre fiction, and her mom, who handed her a romance novel about fifteen years ago and said, "Try it. You'll love it." And Mom was right. Cara's been reading and writing romances ever since! Visit her at www.carasummers.com.

To my niece and godchild Emma Fulgenzi,
who is just the sort of smart, strong, independent
woman I like to write stories about.

May all your Christmas wishes come true—
and then some!

I love you!

Prologue

Washington Post—December 20
Is True Love In the Air?

THE RUBINOV DIAMOND EXHIBIT at the National Gallery has created a lot of excitement in Washington during this holiday season. Although whether people are flocking to see the stone because of its long, sometimes bloody history...or its acclaimed ability to bring lovers together, has yet to be discerned.

The brilliant blue diamond boasts a long and somewhat checkered history. After disappearing for generations, sometimes centuries, it always resurfaces—and always with a new owner. Like other large diamonds, rumors of obsession, murder and theft swirl around it. At one point, it is said that the diamond spent some time in the possession of pirates in the Aegean. More recently in 1999, master jewel thief Arthur Franks was credited with facilitating the Rubinov's reappearance on the market. Neither story has ever been authenticated.

But what seems certain is that whenever the diamond reappears, a new love story is born.

According to the legend, the diamond's power to

ignite an intense attraction between true lovers dates back to ancient times. A few scholars argue the stone originated in Greece, and some even favor the theory that it was Aphrodite, the goddess of love, who first brought the stone to earth and gave it to a mortal she desired above all others.

Its current name, the Rubinov, was bestowed on it in 1917 when Count Peter Rubinov, a close friend of Tsar Nicholas of Russia, fell in love with one of the servants in the royal household and had the diamond made into a necklace for her. Shortly afterward, Count Rubinov, his lover and the necklace disappeared. Many believe it was through the power of the blue stone that they escaped when the Tsar and his family were put to death.

And Count Rubinov's romance isn't the only one. In another story, Helen of Troy was in possession of the stone when Paris first saw her, and it was his irresistible attraction to Helen that compelled him to kidnap her.

Another account claims that Merlin gave the diamond to Guinevere to solidify her relationship with Arthur. Instead, she wore it when she met Lancelot…

In more current stories, it is maintained that the Rubinov played a role in bringing Bonnie and Clyde together before they went on their bank-robbing spree. And though Britain's royal family has always denied it, there are a few insiders who believe the Rubinov was briefly in their possession when Edward first met Mrs. Simpson.

According to my own research, Jacqueline Bouvier photographed it when it was last exhibited in Boston while she was dating John F. Kennedy. The picture she snapped of the necklace is still archived in the John F. Kennedy Library.

But the clincher as far as this reporter is concerned is the number of stories that have crossed my desk since the Rubinov Exhibit opened on December 15. Love is definitely in the air in our nation's Capitol. The latest announcement came from Senator McNeil of Wisconsin, who insists that his daughter met her new fiancé in a chance meeting at the exhibit.

Regina Meyers, spokesperson for Gregory Shalnokov, the reclusive owner of the Rubinov, says Mr. Shalnokov is very pleased his diamond has contributed to the joy of the season.

Clearly, the Rubinov diamond is a matchmaker extraordinaire. This reporter's advice: The clock's ticking. If you want to make the legend of the Rubinov live on, run, don't walk, to the National Gallery. The diamond is scheduled to return to the private collection of Gregory Shalnokov on December 23.

1

POLICE LIEUTENANT Fiona Gallagher looked up from her brochure to survey the crowd waiting to get a look at the legendary Rubinov Diamond.

The long line was being threaded through the exhibition room in a zigzag pattern similar to the ones used for security checks at airports. Her fellow viewers were a diverse group, ranging in age from small children to a couple just ahead of her who appeared to be in their eighties. She'd even spotted a couple of teens dressed in black and wearing red scarves and Santa hats in honor of the season.

Fiona had yet to figure out what the hell she was doing at the exhibition. In the five years she'd lived and worked as a police detective in D.C., she had yet to visit the National Gallery. Two or three times during her wait in line, she'd been tempted to leave. Diamonds with romantic legends surrounding them weren't her cup of tea. True, her boss, Captain Natalie Gibbs-Mitchell, had been nagging her to see it. But Natalie always thought Fiona needed more in her life than just her job. Fiona didn't agree. Her work in the high-profile crime division Natalie ran always gave her the challenges she thrived on.

Perhaps she'd come today out of boredom. She wasn't currently working on a case. That bothered her a bit. Christmas was far from her favorite holiday, and she always depended on her job to get her through the season. But it wasn't like she didn't have things to do. She was running a toy drive at the precinct that would benefit the families of returning vets, and she had a meeting at Walter Reed hospital in less than an hour. After that, she had to make an appearance at a Christmas party, which meant she needed a change of clothes.

The Rubinov hadn't even been on her mind when she'd left the station, but the next thing she knew, her car was at the National Mall. Curiosity had always been one of her strengths as a cop, but it seldom extended beyond the job. And she rarely acted on impulse.

As the couple in front of her moved on, Fiona got her first glimpse of the diamond. And she couldn't seem to drag her gaze away from it. Had she ever seen a stone that blue? Legend aside, she couldn't deny its extraordinary beauty. Even through the glass of the display case, the jewel in the center of the intricately carved necklace burned with a fire that seemed to grow even brighter as she looked at it.

As far as possessing the power to irresistibly draw two people together? Fiona's logical mind balked at that. But she couldn't fault the National Gallery's decision to promote the romantic legend surrounding the stone.

Even in the midst of a busy Christmas season, the Rubinov Diamond had all Washington talking. And not about politics. Several people, including a prominent senator's daughter, had attributed their engagements to the famous stone.

In her experience, true love was a rare thing. She wanted to think that her parents had experienced it, but since she'd lost them when she was four, she had too few memories to rely on. She certainly hadn't spotted anything even resembling true love in the series of foster homes she'd bounced through before she'd entered the police academy.

Although…her captain was very happily married—and expecting her first baby. And Natalie's sisters, Rory and Sierra, were happy in their marriages, too. But in Fiona's view, the former Gibbs sisters were exceptions to the rule.

Was she secretly hoping to find what Natalie and her sisters had found? Was that what had lured her to the exhibition?

Dream on, Fiona. Christmas is a time for broken dreams.

Still, she couldn't quite look away from the diamond, nor could she prevent feeling a little tug of longing.

She had to move on. Putting some effort into it, she tore her gaze away from the Rubinov diamond. It was only then that she noticed a man standing on the other side of the glass case. He was tall and dark haired with broad shoulders. There was something essentially male about him even without taking into account the officer's uniform. She was vaguely aware that an older woman stood to his right, her arm tucked through his. The younger woman to his left said something, and when he smiled, Fiona felt her heart skip a beat.

Now she studied the three people standing directly across from her with the same intensity she'd looked at the diamond. They had their gazes locked on the necklace. Family, she thought. She pushed the tiny twinge of envy away quickly.

Without warning, the officer's eyes lifted and met hers over the display case. For one instant, all she could feel was the impact of his gaze moving through her like a bullet—penetrating first skin, then muscle, blood and bone. Her mind went blank. Except for one word. *Hers.*

She felt a pull and knew only that she wanted to go to him, needed to…

When his gaze shifted back to the older woman at his side, Fiona realized that her heart was beating fast—as if she'd just raced to the top of a hill. And one of her hands had fastened onto the velvet rope in front of her. To hold on? To tear it away?

She could have sworn the fire in the diamond glowed more fiercely.

Ridiculous. She ordered herself to draw in a deep breath and let it out. This wasn't like her at all. And the officer— whoever he was—was a complete stranger.

Icy panic shot up her spine. She shouldn't have come here. It was always a mistake to wish for more than you could have. Without a backward glance at either the diamond or the man, she whirled away. Crumpling the brochure that told about the legend, she stuffed it into her coat pocket and barely kept herself from running out of the exhibition room.

Joy to the world...

The music poured out of the speakers in the sculpture garden at the National Mall, mixing with the chatter and laughter of skaters as they circled the ice rink. Usually, Army Captain D. C. Campbell loved Christmas music.

The song playing right now was a particular favorite. He'd always believed that spreading and receiving joy was the purpose, the mission of Christmas. But this year, he had to admit, the spirit of the season had eluded him. Not even the lights winking merrily on the National Mall were helping. Nor did the sight of his mother and younger sister, Darcy, skating arm in arm as they rounded the corner of the rink.

Using his cane to wave at them, D.C. gave himself a mental shake and turned to walk down the path toward Madison Drive. He knew exactly what his problem was—and he needed to solve it. He was bored out of his mind.

After his last tour of duty in Iraq, running the military police unit at nearby Fort McNair was as exciting as watching paint dry. It was a small base and occupied a scenic location in the Southwest section of the capital. The Anacostia River bordered it on the south and the Washington Channel on the west. The National Defense University was housed on the grounds, and D.C.'s main job was to oversee security. No problem there—since it ran like a well-oiled machine. Handling security had been a tad more challenging in Baghdad.

The other part of his job at Fort McNair was to investigate any crimes committed by personnel assigned to the base. So far the most exciting thing he'd done in the six months he'd been assigned there was to referee a fight that had broken out in the Officer's Club.

Again, it was pretty easy work compared to what he'd done in Iraq. The upside was that it was risk free. You didn't have to second-guess any decisions when you were signing requisition orders. No one's life was on the line. Not his. Certainly not a partner's.

He still felt guilty when he thought of David Eisley, the young private who'd been with him when he'd taken the hit to his leg. The soldier who hadn't survived. But he was dealing with it. Risks, wins and losses—they were part of the job. Part of what had driven him to join the military in the first place.

At other times in his life, D.C. had embraced boredom. After a particularly rough day in a combat situation, a little tedium was welcome. Refreshing even. But enough was enough.

No doubt it was his state of mind that had fueled his imagination earlier that afternoon, when he and Darcy and his mom had been viewing the Rubinov Diamond. That had to have been why he'd had such an…odd reaction to that woman.

When he'd first met her eyes, the tightening in his gut had been unexpected. Raw and hot and sexual. That he might have been able to explain away. After all, she was a beautiful woman. The whiskey-colored eyes and the cameo face framed in a long fall of dark hair was enough to whet the appetite of any male with a pulse. And when she'd turned and strode away, the closer look he'd gotten at her body hadn't disappointed him. Despite the fact she'd been wearing a short jacket and slacks, he'd gotten a clear impression of a lean, athletic body and miles of leg. Desire had punched through him again. Understandable. Enjoyable. But the intense and possessive urge he'd had to follow her was more than surprising. It was unprecedented.

He'd very nearly deserted his family to run after her. As it was, he hadn't been able to take his eyes off of her until she'd disappeared.

What would have happened if he *had* followed his mystery woman? The very nice fantasy that filled his mind helped him to fight off the increasing chill in the air as he continued down the path. The temperature had dropped steadily ever since the sun had set. But while they might warm him, distract him even, it was going to take more than interesting and pleasurable sexual fantasies to solve his current problem.

All he wanted for Christmas was an adventure. Was that too much to ask? Not anything major…he wouldn't wish a crime spree on his base. But he desperately needed something to jar him out of his mind-numbing state.

Thanks to the leg injury he'd suffered on his last tour of duty, it wasn't likely that he was going to see combat action anytime soon. Hell, he couldn't even join his mother and younger sister on the ice rink. Pausing, he turned back to watch the skaters. He barely needed the cane anymore, and the leg itself was at eighty to eighty-five percent mobility. The problem was it wasn't going to get to one hundred. His general had already had a conversation with him about transferring to a desk job at the Pentagon.

Problem was, a desk job didn't appeal to D.C. any more than continuing on at the less-than-exciting Fort McNair.

D.C. tapped his cane impatiently against the ground as he watched his mother and Darcy skate by again. He'd always thought he'd be a military career man just as his father had been. At least that had been his father's plan before he'd been killed in Bosnia. But a career in the army was out if D.C. had to spend the rest of his life on the fringes as he was doing today.

It came upon a midnight clear…

The lilting music had D.C. narrowing his eyes. Who said he had to wait until midnight for a little clarity? There was no time like the present. When January 15 rolled around, instead of signing up for another five years in the army, he could always resign. So what if he didn't know exactly what he'd do next?

His older brother, who owned a security firm in Manhattan, had offered him a job. But in the last year, Jase had taken on a new partner and more recently a wife. No matter. D.C. would figure out something. He always did. The corners of his mouth lifted in a grin. He did like surprises. Wasn't it the predictability of his daily routine at Fort McNair that was driving him nuts?

Having made the decision, something eased inside of him. Finally.

This time, as his mother and sister rounded the curve, he smiled and waved at them. It was his day off, and he'd invited them to join him at the National Mall for some museum touring followed by skating at the sculpture garden. The visit to the National Gallery had been designed to tempt his mother into town. For the last twenty years, ever since Nancy Campbell had stepped into the job of single parent, he'd never known her to take much time off for herself.

So when she'd mentioned she'd love to see the Rubinov Diamond exhibit, D.C. had lost no time planning the day. According to the press releases, the Rubinov boasted a Cupid-like reputation of bringing together those who came in contact with it. But it was nearly equally famous for its history of frequently disappearing for long periods of time. When it invariably resurfaced, it was never possible to trace the relationship between the old owner and the new one.

It didn't require highly trained investigatory skills to assume that there was often some sort of skulduggery afoot. D.C. suspected the diamond had, at various times, gone underground into someone's private collection. He'd learned a lot about the temptations of private collectors when he'd been investigating an art theft case in Iraq, one that had involved some high-level military officials. It had been messy.

Who knew how long the Rubinov had been in the possession of its current owner, Gregory Shalnokov? The reclusive billionaire had admitted to owning it for the past ten years, but just how he'd come to acquire it was shrouded in mystery. D.C. knew that provenances could be forged.

Still, he figured he owed Shalnokov one when he'd seen the look on his mother's and sister's faces as they'd gazed at the diamond. D.C. shook his head. There was something about women and diamonds.

As far as he was concerned, the blue stone was just another rock, albeit one that supposedly had extraordinary powers. Truth told, he'd been more intrigued by the security on both the exhibition room and the display case than he'd been by the diamond. After a fair bit of prompting and a flash of his ID, one of the guards, a man named Bobby, had told him that the lock on the case was voice activated. Only Shalnokov could open it.

Interesting.

Over the years, the legendary diamond had attracted as many thieves as lovers. The article in the *Washington Post* had even mentioned the name of master thief Arthur Franks as having once had possession of the stone. While the female members of D.C.'s family had oohed and aahed over the diamond, he'd been wondering how a good thief might work a successful heist. And the fact that his mind had wandered down that path was pathetic proof of the level of his boredom.

Then he'd glanced up and looked into his mystery woman's eyes. And for those next few seconds, he'd been unaware of anything but her. He couldn't recall ever being that intensely aware of anyone before.

When his cell phone rang, D.C. glanced at the ID and grinned. Jase had been checking in with him once a week since he'd been assigned to Fort McNair. A classic case of big-brotheritis.

"Don't you have something better to do?" D.C. asked.

"As a matter of fact, I do. But Maddie wanted me to call and remind you that you're joining us for Christmas in the Big Apple."

"And you don't think I'm getting daily reminders of that from Mom?"

Jase laughed. "Okay. I'll have to think up better excuses for calling. How are you?"

"I'm fine," D.C said. "Really." And he realized it was the truth. He was okay with the fact that his life after January 15 was a clean slate—something he had plenty of time to write on. It would be an adventure. And after all, wasn't that what he was craving?

"You'll figure something out."

"I will," D.C. said. He would.

Have yourself a merry little Christmas…

The song poured out of the speakers as D.C. pocketed his cell phone. His smile widened. The music seemed louder, the lights brighter, the evening merrier. He was still grinning and watching the skaters when he caught a movement in his peripheral vision. Turning, he spotted a figure at the far end of the garden just inside one of the entrance gates. The lights were focused on the ice rink, but he could still make out the white fur trim on the Santa hat as the person dodged behind one of the trees.

Earlier, when they'd arrived at the National Gallery, there'd been a couple of young people wearing red scarves and Santa hats in the museum. 'Twas the season, D.C. supposed.

He kept his eyes on the festive figure as he darted to the next tree. Intrigued by the furtiveness of the movement, D.C. stepped onto the grass using trees and sculptures for cover as he zigged and zagged away from the ice rink.

Suddenly, the person ducked down along one side of the largest sculpture—the four-sided pyramid. Hiding, D.C. decided. But from what? The question had barely formed in his mind when a second figure suddenly appeared on another side of the sculpture and moved stealthily toward the first. Both figures were dressed alike—dark clothing, a Santa hat and a scarf.

In spite of the dim lighting, D.C. caught the glint of light on metal and watched. The second one raised his arm and springing forward, brought a gun down hard on the other one's head.

D.C. pulled out his revolver as he broke into a run. "Stop. Police."

The person holding the gun whirled and raised his weapon just as uneven ground made D.C. stumble and fall. He landed hard on his bad leg. Dispassionately, he heard a whiny thud and watched a chunk of bark hit the grass inches in front of him. Close, D.C. thought as he rolled to the other side of a tree. Very close.

Still on the ground, he ignored the pain in his thigh and took aim with his own weapon. But the figure was already racing away. The sidewalks on either side of the garden were still filled with tourists, and firing a shot would be too risky.

Hauling himself to his feet, D.C. dialed 911 and relayed his situation as he ran haltingly in the direction the armed man had taken. He exited the gate in time to see a figure wearing a Santa hat disappear into the backseat of an unmarked van. The Mall was lit brightly enough for him to see that there were two other people in the vehicle, one behind the wheel and another in the passenger seat.

The engine roared and tires squealed as the van raced away toward Fourth Street and peeled around the corner. It would be useless to give chase, D.C. thought. Even if his leg had been at one hundred percent, the van was moving too fast. He rubbed his thigh. Now that the adrenaline was fading, the sharpness of the pain was coming through. Loud and clear.

He turned back, and as he limped across the ground toward the fallen figure, he caught a few glimpses of the ice rink. Thanks to the volume of the music and the fact that the person with the gun had used a silencer, the skaters seemed blissfully unaware of the little shoot-out. He leaned down to retrieve his cane and then continued toward the figure on the ground.

The man was lying on his side, one arm flung out, a red

scarf obscuring his features. D.C. knelt down beside the body. It was the hand that caught his attention first. The fingers were long, slender and delicate-looking. He checked for a pulse, found it steady. Carefully drawing the scarf aside, he confirmed his suspicion—this was a woman.

And he knew her.

Lying before him was Private Amanda Hemmings, General Eddinger's administrative assistant at Fort McNair. Small world, D.C. thought.

Examining the fallen woman more closely, he noted the gash on the back of her head oozing blood. And the bruise on her forehead told him she'd hit it, as well, when she fell. He took her hand and patted it. "Private Hemmings?"

No response.

"Amanda?"

Silence again. She'd obviously been hit hard. Above the music from the rink, D.C. caught the faint sound of a siren.

What was Private Amanda Hemmings doing here wearing a Santa hat and red scarf? And why had someone attacked her?

It was a puzzle—and D.C. loved them. He was taking out his notebook and pen when he saw it—just two or three links of gold sticking out of one of the pockets in her jacket. But he'd seen those chain links before. Very carefully, he drew them out.

Excitement surged through him. There hanging at the end of the necklace was the Rubinov diamond.

BAH! HUMBUG!

Though she didn't utter them aloud, the words blinked on and off like a neon sign in Fiona's mind. Impatient and annoyed, she tapped her fingers on the steering wheel of her car while she waited for a group of tourists to climb aboard the bus she'd been following down Constitution Avenue.

Even though it was nearly five forty-five and the sky had darkened over half an hour ago, the traffic around the National Mall hadn't let up. She shouldn't have taken this route. But she hadn't quite been able to put that officer out of her mind. What was even more annoying was that each time she thought about him, the feelings she'd experienced returned—the shortness of breath, the rapid pulse. How could she be so intensely attracted to a total stranger?

She'd succeeded in coming up with a rational explanation for the…unsettling experience. It had been a combination of all the media hype around the diamond together with the Christmas season with its promises of wishes coming true. Add to that the fact that she was at loose ends because she wasn't in the middle of a case, and it made sense that her imagination would react in such a strange way to the diamond…and the army officer.

And damn it, while she'd been thinking of him, her car had somehow found its way to the National Mall. Again.

She spared a glance for the tourists who had formed a line on the sidewalk that ran behind the sculpture garden next to the National Gallery. She seemed to be the only one in a hurry to get somewhere. She stared at them, willing them to pick up the pace as they slowly boarded their bus. It didn't work.

Great! Fiona clamped down on the urge to lean on her horn. It wasn't the bus driver's fault that she was late. Nor could she blame him for the traffic snarl or because she was on her way to an obligatory Christmas party that she'd done her best to get out of.

Her boss, Natalie Gibbs-Mitchell, had refused to take no for an answer. And the fact that her captain was expecting a baby any day added what Fiona felt was a lot of unfair pressure.

When her cell phone rang, Fiona glanced at the caller ID. *Speak of the devil…*

"Don't even think of chickening out on me," Natalie said.

"I swear I'm on my way. I'm running late because I stopped by the National Gallery earlier today and saw the diamond."

"And?"

"You're right. It's beautiful." But it wasn't an image of the necklace that filled her mind. It was the face of the stranger she'd seen over the display glass—that lean face with the ruggedly handsome features.

"And now that you've seen it, what do you think of the legend?"

When she felt the little flutter of panic, Fiona ruthlessly shoved it down. "I think the legend is making this one of the most popular exhibitions ever."

Then she changed the subject. "I'm also running late because my meeting at Walter Reed hospital took longer than I expected."

There was a beat of silence. "And that would be my fault?"

Fiona could picture Natalie on the other end of the call, her expression cool, her brows raised. The image made Fiona smile. "If the shoe fits…"

It had been her captain who'd put her in charge of the department's Christmas toy drive. But it had been her own idea to recruit volunteers to patrol the high-traffic tourist attractions in D.C. In each location, they handed out brochures explaining the drive and describing where and how to drop off toys.

The response had been phenomenal. She glanced beyond the line of tourists. Even now, one of her volunteers might be passing out brochures somewhere on the streets that connected the Smithsonian museums. In spite of her aversion to all things Christmas, she was enjoying the chance to give a needy kid a better Christmas than she'd had.

"Everything's quiet at the station. I checked," Natalie said.

"Me, too." Fiona was on duty tonight and she'd been hoping for a mugging or an assault. No such luck.

She had the police band radio on in the hope of a last-minute reprieve. There'd been a rash of snatch and runs plaguing the Georgetown area. Heck, she'd even settle for a domestic disturbance. It wasn't that Fiona wanted a murder to investigate on the Friday before Christmas, but a little mayhem would have been perfect.

Along the sidewalk, the line of tourists seemed to be getting longer instead of shorter.

"You can't work all the time, Fiona."

"I know." Natalie was hosting a Christmas party at the Blue Pepper, a popular bistro in Georgetown, and Fiona knew most of the people who would be there. More than that, she liked them—her colleagues, Natalie's sisters, their husbands and friends.

It was the Christmas part that bothered her. As far as she was concerned, the best part of the holiday season was being able to put it behind her for another year.

"Fair warning. Now that you've been to see the Rubinov, Chance will probably grill you about its security."

Fiona closed her eyes and bit back a sigh. Natalie's husband, Chance, investigated high-profile art and jewelry thefts for an insurance company, and he'd consulted on the security setup for the Rubinov. So it only made sense that he'd want to get her take on how well the protection was holding up, given the crowds of people who'd been in to see it. At least, that had been one of the reasons Natalie had used when she'd nagged Fiona to go see the diamond.

But she hadn't paid one bit of attention to the security while she'd been in that exhibition room. She'd been too caught up in the stone…and the man…

Ruthlessly, she once more shoved the image of the stranger's face out of her mind. Ahead of her, the bus began to move.

"How much longer will you be?" Natalie asked.

Forever, Fiona thought. *Please.* She knew very well that wishes weren't always granted at Christmas, but maybe…just this once. All she wanted was a case—one that would last through the holidays.

The bus in front of her coughed up exhaust and began to crawl forward.

"I'm moving now," she said. "My ETA is twenty minutes."

"I'll hold you to that," Natalie said and disconnected.

The call came through as she was inching her way toward Ninth Street. Shots fired in the sculpture garden at the National Mall. She was only a couple of football fields away. *Thank God.*

Punching a number into her cell, she pulled onto a grass verge at the same time as she told the dispatcher she was nearly on the scene. Then she plucked her gun out of her evening bag and ran toward the well-lit ice rink.

2

D.C. FELT THE PRESENCE of the other person before he saw or heard a thing. And he sensed danger. Neither surprised him. Combat experience honed a man's perceptions. He didn't glance up from the notes he was taking and didn't slow the movement of his pen, but all his other senses went on full alert.

He was pretty sure that it wasn't the man who'd taken a shot at him. Private Hemmings's assailant had been too intent on escape. D.C. couldn't hear anything other than the still-approaching sirens and the music from the ice rink. Still he felt the threat increase with each passing second. He'd only felt this way one other time. It had been in Baghdad. And he'd learned later that he'd been in the crosshairs of a high-powered rifle.

He let his gaze slide to his gun, which he'd set on the ground. His cane lay next to it. Either one would prove a useful weapon…if he could get to them in time.

"Don't even think about it."

D.C. let out a breath he hadn't known he'd been holding. The voice was husky, authoritative and definitely female. It also meant business.

"D.C. police. Raise your hands and keep them where I can see them."

D.C. did as he was told. As he lifted his gaze, the first thing he saw was the shoes. Cops were wearing interesting footwear these days. Hers were expensive-looking with killer heels and they were moving purposefully toward him. They should have slowed her down, but they didn't. A black coat that flared out as she moved revealed a short red dress and legs that made his gaze want to linger. But the gun she held professionally in both hands was a bit distracting, especially since it was aimed at his most vital organ.

The moment he saw her face, recognition slammed into him like a bare-fisted punch. It was her. His mystery woman. Her face was as striking as he remembered. Delicate features and porcelain-colored skin contrasted sharply with a stubborn chin and a slash of cheekbones that suggested strength. A cop's strength?

Finally, he met her eyes head-on. He registered their color—aged whiskey. Then his cataloging slammed to a halt as he experienced the same raw, primitive desire he'd experienced earlier.

Evidently, lightning could strike twice. His eyes narrowed as she stopped in front of him. He was pretty sure that the danger he'd sensed earlier had nothing to do with the gun and everything to do with the woman.

Who the hell was she?

"PUT YOUR HANDS UP." Fiona was happy to see that her weapon was steady. Because *she* wasn't steady at all. From the first moment she'd spotted him kneeling next to the body, she'd recognized him. And she'd experienced the same intense, impulsive urge to go to him that she'd felt earlier. Instead, she'd halted in her tracks and taken a moment to gather herself before she'd moved toward him.

The 911 caller had identified himself as being in the

military police and had promised to stay on the scene. The gun on the ground next to him and the way he was scribbling in that notebook suggested he was a cop. Still, she'd have to make sure. That was when he'd glanced up and met her eyes. She'd very nearly stopped dead in her tracks again.

Who the hell was he? And how could he have this kind of effect on her?

"Mind if I use my cane?"

"Just give the gun a wide berth."

"I called this in. The victim here is a woman. She's taken a blow to the back of the head and she may have hit her forehead on the edge of the sculpture when she fell. She's unconscious. Her breathing and pulse are steady."

As he spoke, he rose in a smooth series of movements that told Fiona he'd practiced it often. She noticed more details than she had in their earlier encounter. He was larger than she remembered, well over six feet with broad shoulders and a swimmer's body that went well with his lean face. But it was his eyes that grabbed her attention.

Again.

They were the darkest gray she'd ever seen. His gaze was direct and very intense. Not much slipped by those eyes, she could tell. And staring into them was a mistake. The pull he seemed to effortlessly exert on her tightened, and she barely kept herself from walking into his arms.

Impatience bubbled up. She had a job to do, and she would think of how he affected her…later. Better still, she wouldn't think of him at all. "You want to tell me the rest of what you know, Sergeant?"

"It's Captain D. C. Campbell." He moved a hand toward his pocket, then paused. "I have ID."

Which she should have asked for already. "Go ahead."

As she inspected it, he continued, "I'm currently stationed at Fort McNair running the military police unit. It's my day off, and I'm here on an outing with my mother and sister. They're skating."

Fiona thought of the two women she'd seen with him in the exhibition and recalled her impression that they'd been related.

Narrowing her eyes, she slipped her revolver into her evening bag. "You want to get to the good part?"

"Sure thing." Humor flashed in his eyes.

Even as she knelt beside the body to verify the pulse, the sirens stopped. D. C. Campbell kept his report on the altercation between the two people he'd observed detailed, yet concise. One person had mugged another person on the National Mall.

"Did her attacker get away with anything?"

"No. He took one shot at me, then seemed to lose his nerve."

The woman was lying half on her side, her face in profile, and something tugged at the edge of Fiona's mind. She located a wallet and was about to check the victim's ID when he said, "I know her."

She glanced up at him. "Who is she?"

"She's my general's administrative assistant—Private Amanda Hemmings."

A memory clicked into place in Fiona's mind. She remembered the young blonde woman in uniform who'd stepped into her office, bubbling with enthusiasm, so eager to help with the toy drive. Fiona frowned down, first at the ID and then at the woman. She still looked young and very defenseless. Something tightened around her heart. "I know her, too. I only met her once. She's one of the volunteers helping with the D.C. Police Department's toy drive. That's the reason she's wearing the Santa hat. The hats were her idea. All my volunteers are wearing them."

"The man who attacked her was wearing one, too."

Spotting two uniforms hurrying toward them, Fiona frowned, then rose, pulled out her ID and held it out to them. But she never took her eyes off of D.C. "He was wearing a hat, too? That's odd. I wonder what was behind the attack."

"I have a clue."

When he pulled the necklace out of his pocket, she stared. Even in the dim light, the large blue diamond in the pendant glowed. Without thinking, she cupped her hands and held them out. "It's the Rubinov, isn't it?"

"That would be my guess."

As he placed it in her hands, his fingers brushed against her palm. It was a momentary contact—accidental, casual. But Fiona felt the impact—a stirring mix of heat, pleasure and promise—right down to her toes. Closing her fingers over the necklace, twin impulses grabbed her. One to step forward, the other to turn and run.

Out of the corner of her eye she saw two medics hurrying toward them with a stretcher. But before she turned to deal with them, she met D. C. Campbell's eyes again. There was a heat in them that nearly matched the fiery glow in the center of the diamond. There was no physical contact between them anymore, but her skin still burned where his fingers had brushed against it. Neither of them moved.

"Interesting," he said, letting his gaze drop briefly to the stone, which she still held in her outstretched palm. "You're aware of the legend."

"I am." She had to push the words through a very dry throat, and the effort had her lifting her chin. "I believe in legends about as much as I believe in Santa Claus."

"It will be interesting to see where this leads."

Nowhere, Fiona thought as she fought a pump of panic. But

she didn't say the word aloud. Instead she turned her attention to the medics. She'd handle D. C. Campbell later.

OH, IT WOULD DEFINITELY lead somewhere, D.C. thought. Two people didn't experience the kind of connection they'd just felt and walk away from it.

D.C. stepped away from Amanda Hemmings, giving the medics room to check her over. The older of the two, a plump woman in glasses, glanced at him. "You find her?"

"I saw it happen," D.C. said. "She was struck on the head from behind with a gun and fell down hard. Looks like she hit her head on the edge of the sculpture. She's been out ever since."

"Good to know." The woman went back to her job.

D.C. glanced over at the ice rink. From his position, he could see that some of the skaters had lined up along the edge, their curiosity aroused by the sirens and the flashing lights. One of the uniforms was taping off the scene while two others were keeping those still strolling along the Mall from entering at the other side of the garden. He couldn't see either his mother or his sister, although he would soon, he suspected. Once they spotted him in the middle of this, they'd be right over.

Taking out his cell, he punched in the number of his general, Myra Eddinger. While he filled her in on what he knew so far, he kept his gaze on the mystery woman who'd taken charge of the crime scene. She radiated competence the way she radiated sensuality. Even at a distance of twenty or so feet, the intensity of the pull he'd felt when he'd first seen her still hummed and sizzled like an electric current in his blood.

"You're sure the necklace is the Rubinov?" General Eddinger asked.

"Either that or an excellent copy."

"Best guess," Eddinger demanded.

"It's the real McCoy." His gaze never wavered from his mystery woman because it was what he was feeling for her that was fueling his certainty. He wasn't totally sure he bought into the legend, either. But something was definitely happening between them. If the necklace hadn't been involved, he might have chalked what he was experiencing—what they were experiencing—up to some really excellent chemistry.

But he could have sworn that the blue stone had brightened when he'd placed it in her hand—just as it had brightened in the display case when he'd first seen her.

And when his fingers had brushed briefly against her palm, what he'd experienced had gone beyond desire to something that bordered on recognition.

She shot a look his way, and the moment their eyes met, everything else faded. General Eddinger's voice became a hum in his ear. The faces of those standing on the edges of the scene blurred. And the light dimmed as if he were on a stage set. In that instant, there was only her.

He was only released from the spell when she turned away and put her cell phone to her ear.

"Are you still there, Captain Campbell?"

"Yes. Our connection faded just for a moment," he lied.

"If you're right on this, then Private Hemmings has played some role in the attempted theft of the century. Everything I know about her tells me she wouldn't have done anything purposely to steal that diamond. I want to know just how it ended up in her pocket. So I'm going to make a few phone calls and arrange for you to work along with the Washington police on this case. I'll expect you to get to the bottom of it."

"Yes, sir." And that's what he should be focusing on. But

for a moment his thoughts were directed on the woman he would now be working with. Knowledge was always power.

She wasn't as tall as he'd first thought. Maybe five foot four without the killer heels. And then there were those legs. Looking at them for more than a few seconds was enough to stimulate some very interesting fantasies. The current one was generating enough heat to keep him toasty warm.

D.C. gave himself a mental shake. She was still distracting him from more important things—such as following General Eddinger's orders. If what he suspected was true, the Rubinov diamond must have been stolen from its display case shortly after the exhibition had closed at 5:00 p.m. He and his family had been in the last group to view the necklace.

It must have been almost five as they'd followed crowds toward the exit doors. He searched his mind for the details of what he'd seen as they made their way out. The one thing he did recall was a tall woman with straight blond hair having a heated conversation with an older woman and a group of youngsters. As they'd passed by, his mother had frowned. When he'd asked her about her reaction, she'd said that the blonde was acting like a bully. Some of the kids had needed to use the bathrooms, but the woman had been adamant that the restrooms were closed.

D.C. smiled as he recalled the incident. Nancy Campbell had strong ideas about how children should be treated.

Afterward, they'd come directly to the sculpture garden and his mother and Darcy had gone in to get skates. No alarm had sounded.

D.C. shifted his gaze to Amanda Hemmings as she was being carried away to a waiting ambulance. How in the world had she ended up with the Rubinov diamond in her pocket?

"Lieutenant?" It was a seasoned-looking man in a uniform

who called out, and D.C.'s mystery woman strode toward him. The man had to have at least fifteen years on his lieutenant, and though D.C. couldn't catch what they were saying, there was an ease in the way they communicated that suggested respect on each side.

So she was a lieutenant. And he didn't even know her name. Amusement moved through him. He was definitely slipping. Putting all his years of investigative training to use, D.C. managed to extract not only her name, but a little background information, as well, from one of the uniformed men taping off the area.

Her name was Fiona Gallagher. She'd been working in Washington for five years, she was well respected, and she had a reputation for doing everything by the book. Before that, she'd worked in Atlanta. She'd been transferred to Washington specifically to work in the high-profile crime unit. D.C. stored the information away, then shifted his position so that he could lean against one of the sculptures. His leg deserved a little TLC after his abortive run after the armed man. But the initial pain he'd felt was already easing.

Finally, he refocused his mind back on the diamond. Of course, the necklace that he'd taken from Amanda Hemmings's pocket could be a fake. His gut instinct aside, its authenticity would have to be checked out—the sooner the better.

He knew someone who might be able to help with that—an insurance investigator who just happened to make his home in Georgetown. It had been five years ago when he and Chance Mitchell had worked together to close down a highly efficient art theft ring in Baghdad, and he'd been meaning to look the man up.

And he needed to know more about Amanda Hemmings. Since he was going to be stuck in the sculpture garden for a while, D.C. decided that he'd put his brother to work. He'd learned from experience just how efficient the men at Campbell and Angelis Security were at running background checks.

As he punched in a number, D.C. cast another long look at Lieutenant Fiona Gallagher's long legs.

"YOU SAID YOUR ETA was twenty minutes," Natalie said. "That was almost an hour ago."

Fiona swore silently as she glanced at her watch. "Sorry, I should have called sooner."

The fact that her captain's voice was threaded with concern rather than annoyance had Fiona mentally kicking herself. She hurried to give Natalie a detailed report on what had delayed her.

What she didn't relay was why she hadn't wound things up at the crime scene as quickly as she should have. Captain D. C. Campbell was distracting her. Each and every time she'd scanned the area or the faces of the curiosity junkies who'd gathered along the crime scene tape, her eyes had returned to him. Once she'd even caught him gazing back at her, and she'd felt that same mind-numbing flash of heat. That fact alone was enough to tempt her to look at him again—just to see if his effect on her was diminishing.

So far it wasn't.

"So let me summarize," Natalie said. "One of our toy drive volunteers was the victim of a mugging at the National Mall. We don't know who her assailant was except that he, too, was wearing a Santa hat. Nor do we know who his two pals in the van were. And it looks like the four of them may have tried to pull off the heist of the century by stealing the Rubinov diamond right out of the National Gallery."

Fiona frowned. "The question is how?"

"Chance will be all over the how part."

"I'm betting they had inside help. How else could anyone get a well-guarded diamond out of the National Gallery without setting off an alarm? Maybe Amanda and/or her assailant were just supposed to bring it out of the gallery. Who would suspect a toy drive volunteer?"

"And Hemmings decided at the last minute to take the diamond and run?" Natalie asked.

"Or she had a change of heart?" In her mind, Fiona could almost see Natalie in the middle of a party at the Blue Pepper, jotting the possibilities down in her notebook. In the background she could hear chatter and Christmas music.

"I need to talk to her," Fiona said. "The medics weren't able to bring her around before they transported her."

"Hemmings's involvement could cause some public relations problems for the army," Natalie murmured.

"Yes."

"I have to say I'm a bit jealous. If I weren't so close to my due date, I'd be tempted to work at your side on this one." She paused. "So, what do you think of your Captain Campbell? Is he good?"

"Yeah," Fiona said. She had to give him that much. She scanned the area again, playing back the scene D.C. had described. If what had happened here was some kind of a falling-out among thieves, it was thanks to him that they had the diamond.

But she could see the direction Natalie was heading in. "I don't need a partner."

"The army is going to want in on this," Natalie said briskly. "First, we'll have to make sure what you have is the real Rubinov." There was a beat of silence. "Hold on. I've got a call coming in from the commissioner. It never ceases to amaze me how fast news travels in our nation's Capitol."

Politics. Fiona bet she knew exactly what the call from the commissioner was about—and that her boss had seen it coming. The army was going to want in on the investigation. They had a right, Fiona supposed.

Whirling, she narrowed her gaze on D. C. Campbell. He'd evidently been a busy boy while she'd been directing traffic and gathering information. In less than an hour, he'd reported to someone who'd gotten the commissioner's ear. Not an easy feat to pull in the last few days before Christmas.

He was standing over near the ice rink, and he'd been joined by the same two women she'd seen with him earlier in the exhibition room. Both were tall and striking-looking and bore a strong family resemblance to Campbell. As if they had a will of their own, Fiona's eyes strayed to D. C. Campbell. Even now when he wasn't gazing directly at her, there was still that little skip of her pulse to deal with.

"Fiona, are you still there?"

Dammit! Disgusted with herself, Fiona turned away and refocused her attention on Natalie. "I'm here."

"The commissioner got a call from a General Eddinger at Fort McNair. The bad and the good news, depending on your perspective, is that you're going to be working this case with Captain Campbell."

"Figures." It was logical that they work together. And Fiona didn't like to waste time fighting logic.

"The army does have a right to run their own investigation," Natalie said.

"But it would be more efficient if we worked together."

"Exactly. I can hear the lack of enthusiasm in your voice, but I learned during the few times I've worked with Chance that two heads are often better than one."

"You've worked with Chance?" It was common knowledge

around the department that Natalie and her sisters were daughters of a professional thief. But Natalie had never before mentioned that she and Chance had worked together.

"Ancient history—back when we first met. We were paired up for the first time on a high-profile case for the department. After that, I worked undercover with him on a case on my own time. Our mission was to steal back a diamond. We fell in love on the job."

Another pump of panic had Fiona placing a hand against her chest just where she'd tucked the Rubinov away for safe keeping. *She had to get a grip.*

"Now—" Natalie's tone turned brisk "—I want you to bring the diamond and your Captain Campbell to the Blue Pepper."

Fiona frowned. "I was going to go to the hospital and check on Private Hemmings."

"I'll send a couple of uniforms over there to keep us updated. By the time you get here, Chance will locate someone who can authenticate the Rubinov."

When Natalie disconnected, Fiona frowned down at the phone. She could tell that D. C. Campbell was looking at her by the tingle of awareness that moved through her. The nip in the night air contrasted sharply with the heat that shot through her veins. It was as if his mere presence heightened all of her senses. And she was stalling. Logic was one thing. Her reaction to D. C. Campbell was another.

It wasn't that she didn't like men. She did. In the right time and place. So far, she'd been able to keep them on the fringes of her life. Enjoyable, but not essential. And she wanted to keep it that way.

Gut instinct warned her that Captain Campbell was not a man kept easily in his place. Already, he'd slipped into her mind and was staging an assault on her senses.

Not that she was going to admit it had anything to do with the Rubinov or its legend. What she was feeling was just a trick of chemistry. There'd been a time in her life when she'd had stars in her eyes and she'd believed in wishes and dreams. It had been Christmas time then, too. There was something about the season that made her lose track of reality. But she could handle this…situation. She would handle it and D. C. Campbell, as well.

Straightening her shoulders, she raised her gaze to meet his and strode forward.

3

LIEUTENANT FIONA GALLAGHER walked the way she drove—
purposefully and fast. They'd come to Georgetown in separate
cars, so he'd had time to observe the competent way she
threaded her way through Washington traffic. Because of the
season, parking was at a premium. They'd parked their
vehicles several blocks away from the Georgetown bistro
where her boss had summoned them.

She'd said nothing since she'd joined him at his car, where
she'd passed along the news that as soon as Amanda Hemmings had reached the hospital, she'd been rushed in for
X-rays, but hadn't regained consciousness yet. Fiona had delivered the information in a matter-of-fact voice, but if D.C.
read her correctly, she wasn't any happier about the news
than he was. Many of their questions might be answered if
they could just talk to Amanda Hemmings.

In spite of her killer heels, the lieutenant strode along the
sidewalk at a fast clip. For now, D.C. was willing to let the
silence stretch between them.

The twenty-minute drive from the Mall had given him
some time to think about how he was going to handle her. Professionally. General Eddinger had already made the arrangements. Like it or not, he and the lieutenant were going to work
together on this case. The question was, how did he want it

to play out? In his experience, there were two ways to work with a partner: around them or with them. And he bet he knew exactly what choice Fiona Gallagher had already made.

They'd nearly reached a corner when she realized she was outpacing him and slowed down until he caught up.

"Sorry," she murmured.

"No problem."

It wasn't the first example of her thoughtfulness. Earlier at the sculpture garden, she'd arranged for one of the squad cars to drive his mother and sister to Union Station so they could catch the eight o'clock train back to Baltimore.

As they crossed the street, D.C. took her arm and felt her stiffen.

"I don't need help crossing the street, Captain."

"Maybe I do."

The look she shot him was cool and assessing. "I don't think so. You don't impress me as a man who needs much help with anything."

D.C. smiled. "Thanks, but you'd be wrong. I want your help solving this case. And my guess is that you're not happy at the prospect of working with me."

"Your guess is correct. But don't take it personally. I don't have a history of working well with partners." Stepping up on the curb, she turned to face him. "My last one was shot."

Her tone was flat, but D.C. saw the flash of pain in her eyes and understood. "He's alive?"

"Yes. It was a shoulder wound. He'll be returning to work in a few weeks."

"You're lucky. My last partner didn't make it. He died in the same little skirmish that sidelined my leg." The words were out before he could stop them. He hadn't talked about David's death. Hadn't been able to—not even to his family.

"I'm sorry." She reached for his hand, linked her fingers with his.

For a moment, silence stretched between them again. The understanding in her eyes eased the tightness around his heart.

"Let's hope we both have better luck this time," he said finally as she freed her hand and continued to walk. "In the meantime, I think it might be good if we got to know one another. Tell me about yourself."

"I'm a cop."

"C'mon, Lieutenant. You know a lot about me. Turnabout's fair play."

Stopping, she turned to him. "I don't know anything about you."

"You've met my mom and sister. You're practically part of the family. They liked you, by the way. They really appreciated you getting them to Union Station. But showing them the Rubinov—they're not going to forget that."

Nor was he going to forget that moment when she'd pushed her coat aside and pulled the necklace out of the front of her dress. The gesture had left him with a vivid image in his mind of exactly where the diamond had been nestling.

"Next time my big brother calls to check up on me, I'll let you talk to him. Jase is ex-navy and special ops, and he runs a security firm in New York. I called and asked him to run a background check on Amanda Hemmings."

She was studying him now, her eyes narrowed. D.C. had the uncomfortable feeling that he was on a slide under a microscope.

"I'll even tell you my deepest and darkest secret."

Her brows arched. "And that is?"

"What D.C. stands for."

Fiona suddenly felt the corners of her mouth twitch. "I'm not sure I want to know."

"Tell me if you change your mind."

The man was charming. She had to grant him that. And that charm might help while they were questioning suspects. He might prove useful in other ways, too—especially with that brother who could run background checks.

"We can either work around each other or together," he stated.

"True." And on the drive to Georgetown, she'd already decided on the former, hadn't she? She'd put on a good front, cooperate when he asked, and do her own thing.

"Working around each other is going to cost us time. And this is an important case. If we're right and you've got the real Rubinov tucked near your heart, we're dealing with the kind of theft that might have made history—if it had been successful. We need to find out why it didn't work out that way. And how the legendary diamond ended up in Amanda Hemmings's pocket."

"There had to have been someone on the inside."

"Agreed. My brother says that there isn't a security system in the world that can't be hacked into. But it would take a real pro to crack the one at the National Gallery. My gut feeling is that Amanda Hemmings isn't that person."

She nodded. "She was working for or with someone."

"Or she's an innocent pawn," D.C. countered. "In any case, we'll have to look at the owner. Gregory Shalnokov is a very rich man. My experience with the rich is that they're never rich enough. If he puts the stone on display and orchestrates a successful robbery, he gets to have his cake, in this case the Rubinov, and eat it, too, when he collects the insurance money."

Fiona found herself agreeing again. They would have to scrutinize Gregory Shalnokov.

"And to prove that I'll make a valuable partner, I learned

from one of the guards that the display case housing the Rubinov could only be opened with Shalnokov's voice."

She stopped short and turned to stare at him. He hadn't had to tell her that. Not that she wouldn't have eventually discovered it for herself.

As if he read her mind, he said, "If we're going to be partners, it'll save time if we share everything."

"Okay." As the first snowflakes began to fall, the wind stung her cheeks. Turning up her collar, she started down the next block. "Right now, the only suspect we've got is Private Hemmings. That's going to be a PR problem for the army."

"True."

"I'm worried that you might have an agenda—to prove Amanda Hemmings innocent."

"I won't lie to you. That's the outcome my general would prefer."

She slanted him a look. "That could interfere with your objectivity."

"It won't. What about you? You're also going to have a bit of a PR problem if one of your volunteers used her work to help out with the theft."

"That won't keep me from digging out the truth."

"Then we shouldn't have a problem. How's the food at this restaurant we're going to?"

"Excellent. But we're not going there to eat."

D.C. sighed. "A man can dream. What's your captain like?"

"I wouldn't want to spoil your first impression."

"Fair enough."

For half a block, they walked again in silence. And it was oddly companionable, Fiona realized. The street was quiet. At seven-thirty, residents had either left for the night or were celebrating the season with family and friends. Lights twinkled on shrubs, and Christmas trees glowed in the windows.

They were still a hundred yards from the corner when two figures rounded it and headed toward them. They wore jeans and hooded sweatshirts. Both male, Fiona decided. And young. Each was using earphones and one was texting a message. The Georgetown campus was only a short distance, so they could be college kids. But it was a little early on a Friday night to be heading back from one of the watering holes on P Street that students favored.

"Trouble," D.C. murmured.

His instincts were aligned with hers, and adrenaline spiked through her. "A couple of hours ago I was practically praying for a little snatch and run."

"Be careful what you wish for."

The two young men were drawing steadily closer.

"Look." He spoke softly as he slipped his hand around her upper arm. "Let's make it easy for them."

"I'm not giving them my purse."

"Of course not. We just want to throw them off guard. Follow my lead. When I turn you, bring your purse up between us."

Without waiting for a reply, he pulled her close until only her evening bag separated them. Even while she slipped her hand in and grasped her revolver, she was intensely aware of other details. Other sensations. His chest was hard as a rock, and he was taller than she'd thought. In her heels, she still only came up to his chin. His hand was large enough to wrap completely around her arm. Even through her coat sleeve, she could feel the pressure of each one of his fingers. And she was pretty sure she'd need a crowbar to dislodge them.

"What are you..." Her whispered words trailed off as he

bent his head closer. For one instant, she was sure he was going to kiss her. Every nerve in her body went on full alert. She should have moved—pushed him away. But she was helpless against the wave of longing that moved through her. For one instant, she lost track of every thought. All she wanted was to feel his lips against hers.

At the last moment, he angled his head and whispered in her ear. "Can you get your gun out?"

Ruthlessly, she focused. "Already did." They were about to be mugged. In her peripheral vision, she saw a figure crossing the street. "There's one behind us."

"You handle him. On a count of three. One…"

He wasn't giving her any time to argue. The other two were close enough that she could hear their footfalls on the pavement.

"Two…"

She didn't like the plan. She was the one with the gun and he was outnumbered. What if…?

"Three."

Even as she stepped away and brought her revolver up, she angled her stance so that she could keep D.C. and the other two in her peripheral vision. Still she barely caught the flash of movement as the cane struck one of the young men in the arm. He yelped in pain.

"Hands up," she said to the one who'd approached from behind. This close she could see he was young, not more than fifteen or sixteen.

"Whoa." He threw his hands out in front of him as if to ward her off.

Out of the corner of her eye, Fiona saw the cane flash again. This time a startled cry was followed by the sound of something clattering to the sidewalk. Then the two men D.C. had used his cane on turned and fled.

"Don't shoot, lady!" The young man she had her gun aimed at whirled and ran, too.

She pivoted around fully in time to see the other two disappear around the corner. Only then did she lower her weapon and slip it back into her purse.

"Good work," D.C. said.

"No, it wasn't." Anger, relief and annoyance had her voice tightening. "I had the gun. And you were outnumbered."

"All's well that ends well."

It was only then that she saw the revolver lying on the sidewalk. They'd been armed. She never should have agreed... Slipping a hanky out of her pocket, she bent down to retrieve the weapon. "We let them get away."

"They were kids."

"Kids with a gun."

D.C. merely shrugged. "We've got it now, and they'll think twice before they try their little snatch-and-run game again."

"Maybe. Maybe not."

"Relax. It's Christmas. Don't you believe in second chances?"

She met his eyes. "What I believe is that we need to lay down some ground rules if we're going to work together."

"I'm not big on rules."

"I am." Fiona whirled to pace three steps away. Though she had a temper, she prided herself on keeping it in check. When she thought she had it together, she turned back and bumped into him. In the instant before they separated, she felt the sear of flames at every contact point. The intensity of the sensation shocked her, and she wanted badly to turn and run. Ruthlessly, she clamped down on the impulse. "Let me put it this way. You're army. You're used to giving orders. Usually, I'm not so good at taking them."

"Meaning?"

"I should have handled the two coming toward us. You should have taken the one who was alone. But you didn't give me a chance to tell you that. We have very different styles."

His expression sobered as he studied her. "I can't change my style. But you're right. Part of my job in the army is to give orders. I can work on that. I'd even be willing to take turns."

She hadn't expected him to admit anything. Since he had, she felt compelled to add. "In this case your particular style worked."

His smile was slow and engaging. "Admit it. You're really not annoyed because we scared them away instead of arresting them."

She lifted her chin. "We have a bigger case to work on."

"Agreed." He took a strand of her hair and rubbed it between his fingers. They were still standing close together—nearly as close as they'd been when he'd pulled her to him. She felt that knife-edged longing begin to build again.

Above the tang of smoke in the air, she caught the scent of his soap. Basic and wonderfully male. All she had to do was move, take a tiny step forward, and she could experience again the hard press of his body against hers. Just thinking about it had the searing heat returning. Her gaze drifted to his mouth. His lips were thin and very masculine. They would be hard and demanding. And she relived that instant when all she'd wanted was to have his mouth pressed to hers.

"You're worried about what's going on between us," he said.

Oh, yeah, she was worried about it in same distant corner of her mind that wasn't consumed with the desire to frame his face with her hands and drag his mouth to hers.

"You're wondering if it will interfere."

It already was. It was interfering with her ability to think about anything but D. C. Campbell. A sudden surge of impatience helped her regain her balance, and she dragged her gaze away from his mouth. "We're both adults. We can ignore what we're feeling."

The fingers toying with her hair moved to trace the line of her jaw. "I'm not so sure."

As her pulse scrambled, then raced, Fiona once more found her mind in tune with his.

In a lightning-fast move, he thrust his fingers into her hair. "Why don't we test the waters?" he asked as he covered her mouth with his.

Fiona froze as a riot of sensations flooded her system. Her blood pounded, her skin heated, her bones melted. One part of her mind rejoiced. Finally!

She couldn't seem to control the response that sprang out of her, wild and wanton. Her arms wound around him and she pressed closer and closer until every plane and angle of his body was molded to hers.

She felt very small against him, very fragile and gloriously feminine. She relished the unusual sensations. His mouth was so demanding, his taste so dark and compelling. So male. Greedy for more, her tongue moved aggressively against his, seeking, searching. As she heard his moan, felt his heart pump against hers, arousal and excitement shot through her. Never had she felt this alive. Urgency built with such speed, such intensity that she couldn't control it. Didn't want to. There was nothing but him—his arms, his lips, those sleek, hard muscles. Nothing but him.

Test the waters. That's what he'd promised himself when he'd lowered his lips to hers. But he'd expected resistance, anticipated it. Perhaps he'd even wanted it. If she'd just struggled a little, he'd have known how to handle it. But when she'd melted against him, he'd discovered he'd never been in more dangerous territory in his life.

He could drown in her. Willingly. But not quietly. He felt as if he were being sucked into unknown depths by a riptide. This woman could take him places he'd never been. He found the idea intriguing. Irresistible.

The sudden urge to touch her was overwhelming. He wanted to slip his hands beneath her coat and run them up her sides, molding, teasing, tormenting. He imagined slipping his fingers beneath the hem of her dress and moving them up those strong thighs until he found and probed her center. Just the thought had needs exploding violently, painfully.

In some small, rational corner of his mind, D.C. knew that if he started to touch her, he wouldn't be able to stop. But the street was quiet, and fewer than ten paces away, shadows blackened the space between two old Georgetown homes. All he had to do was to draw her into the darkness, and he could have her. He could take her up against the wall of the house before either of them regained their senses. It would be crazy and wild. And wonderful.

Only one thing held him back. The undeniable certainty that she could drain his control away as easily as she could pull the plug on a bathtub full of water. Fear sliced its way through all the other sensations. With it came the same gut feeling of danger that he'd sensed when he'd been taking notes in the sculpture garden. Tearing his mouth free of hers, D.C. drew air into his lungs, hoping it would cool the heat radiating through him. This woman had the power to change his life.

Very carefully, he set her away from him. For a moment, he felt winded, as if he'd raced to the top of a very high cliff.

And he'd very nearly jumped off.

It gave him some satisfaction that she looked as if she, too, had been blindsided by the kiss. Her eyes were dark and clouded, her mouth moist and swollen. And he wanted nothing more than to kiss her again. But if he did…

Clamping down even more tightly on his control, he said, "Fiona, are you all right?"

Admiration filled him as he watched her eyes clear and her focus return. "You…shouldn't have done that."

"Maybe not. But I'm not going to apologize."

Her eyes flashed. "Did I ask for an apology?" She whirled, but he snagged her hand before she could move away.

"Look on the bright side. At least now we know what we're dealing with. We just have to decide what we're going to do about it."

The look she shot him was very cool. "Don't get your hopes up, D.C."

He laughed then and felt a little of his tension ease. "A man can dream, Lieutenant." And he was pretty sure that the dream was going to come true—whether they wanted it to or not.

4

CHRISTMAS LIGHTS TWINKLED everywhere in the Blue Pepper, and there was a gigantic tree close to the table in the bar where Fiona and her boss were seated. The place was filled with the clatter of glasses, the hum of conversation, and threaded through it came the sounds of a live band.

In the main dining room, the Christmas party Natalie was hosting for the department was in full swing. On the way to their table, Fiona had waved at her captain's two sisters, Rory and Sierra, and a few of her colleagues.

A short distance away, D.C. stood with Natalie's husband, Chance Mitchell, at the end of the bar. When Fiona and D.C. had arrived about twenty minutes earlier, she'd learned that Chance and D.C. had worked together four years earlier. She imagined the two men were catching up on old times.

Before they'd retired to the bar, Natalie and Chance had led them into a private office where Chance's gemologist had identified the diamond they'd recovered in the sculpture garden as the Rubinov. Since Chance's company had written the insurance policy, he'd taken custody of the necklace.

She glanced at D.C. and saw him laugh at something Chance had said. The office where the man had examined the diamond had been small, and with five people in it, they'd all been forced to stand shoulder to shoulder. She didn't believe in legends. But there'd been a moment as she'd removed the necklace from the front of her dress when she'd been very aware of D.C. standing next to her and of each and every point where they were in contact. And she'd felt that same intense pull she'd felt when he'd first placed the Rubinov in her hands. Only this time it was even stronger.

"So what role did Amanda Hemmings play in all of this?" Fiona forced her attention back to Natalie.

"Is she a key figure or has she been duped? My sense from my brief chat with General Eddinger is that she's favoring the duped scenario." Natalie had angled her chair so that she could prop up her feet on a neighboring banquette. One hand rested on her belly, the other tapped a pencil on a slim notebook. *Elegant* was the word that always came to Fiona's mind when she thought of her boss. Tonight, Natalie wore her reddish-gold hair up, and in the black silk pant suit, she might have stepped right off the pages of a stylish fashion layout that targeted pregnant moms. "What does your instinct tell you, Fiona?"

"I don't know enough about her yet. When I first saw her lying there on the ground, I didn't recognize her as the young woman who'd walked into my office that day. She'd been so enthusiastic about doing something for the men at Walter Reed, it's hard to believe she'd get involved in something like this. She came up with idea of having all the volunteers wear black with Santa hats and red scarves, as a kind of uniform that would set them apart from all the other volunteers that are asking for donations at this time of year. And yet, she had the necklace in her pocket."

Natalie waited, saying nothing.

"I can theorize and analyze my gut feelings about how the stone got there and why someone hit her over the head in the sculpture garden," Fiona continued. "But the only thing I'm pretty certain of is that she couldn't have done it alone."

"Chance agrees," Natalie said. "He personally oversaw the security setup for the Rubinov exhibit. He believes there had to be someone on the inside. Even a top-notch hacker would have needed information."

"I need to talk to Amanda. The latest news I have is she's still unconscious and they've scheduled her for a CAT scan. They're going to call me as soon as they know more about the extent of her injuries. I'll need a search warrant for her apartment." Fiona opened her purse and flipped open her notebook. "I got the address off the ID in her wallet."

Natalie copied it on the pad in front of her. "I'll put the warrant in the works first thing in the morning. In the meantime, I'll send a patrol car over to keep an eye on the building."

"And the two uniforms you sent to the hospital—can they stay? I think we ought to keep someone on duty outside her room once she's assigned to one."

"You're worried about her."

Fiona lifted, then dropped her shoulders. "There's someone out there who brought a gun down on her head. And he's got two buddies."

"I'll take care of it." Natalie shifted slightly in her chair. "For the moment, only a very few of us know that the Rubinov was stolen. Chance will let the owner know, of course. Chance's company will want answers. If someone has broken through the security at the National Gallery, who's to say they won't try again?"

Pausing, Natalie rubbed her hand over her belly. "Chance will work as closely as he can with you on this, but our little bundle of joy may put in an early appearance and distract him. First thing in the morning, he'll inform key people at the

National Gallery. After that, the news will start leaking to the media. I'd like to keep the spotlight off of exactly how the diamond was recovered for as long as we can."

"The less the thieves know about what we know, the better," Fiona mused.

"Exactly. So…" Natalie closed her notebook and leaned back in her chair. "Since Chance and I could be sidelined at any time, it's more important than ever that you work well with your partner. What do you think of Captain D. C. Campbell?"

Fiona noted that her new partner had snagged himself a plate of food from one of the several laden buffet tables.

"He's resourceful."

"And attractive."

"That, too."

"What else can you tell me about him?"

"He's smart. In spite of the cane, he handles himself well." She told Natalie about the aborted snatch and run. "And if he hadn't driven off the man who attacked Amanda Hemmings, Chance wouldn't be returning the Rubinov to the National Gallery tomorrow morning."

"Smart and resourceful. Those were two of the words Chance used when he described D.C. Unorthodox was another. But Chance says he gets results. My husband wouldn't have stopped the art thefts in Baghdad without his help."

"What did he do?"

Natalie's lips twitched. "He disguised himself as a buyer for some of the art and Chance posed as his gay lover."

Fiona narrowed her eyes on the two men. "They passed as a gay couple."

"Yes. Of course, in his line of work, Chance has run these kinds of cons before. He's very good. But in the Baghdad case, he gives the credit for the success of the operation largely to Campbell. My question is…can you work with him?" Natalie asked. "This is a very high-profile case. Once the media gets wind of the attempted theft, we'll have a PR circus on our hands."

Fiona knew her captain well enough to know that Natalie had sensed the tension between D.C. and her, so she met her boss's eyes. "I'd be a fool not to work with him. He's good. He keeps on top of things. And he has connections. His brother is ex-navy, special ops, and he runs a security firm in Manhattan. D.C. has asked him to run a background check on Amanda Hemmings."

Natalie smiled slowly. "Sounds like he could be a real asset to your investigation. So, you'll find a way to handle your attraction to him."

Fiona swore silently to herself. Her boss was a very perceptive woman. She shifted her gaze to D.C. She was almost getting used to the instant flare of heat she felt each time she did. The aching spurt of hunger was new and no doubt, due to that kiss.

On the walk to the Blue Pepper she'd nearly succeeded in pushing the kiss out of her mind. Thinking about it only made her head spin. First she'd tried to convince herself that D.C.'s effect on her senses must have been an aberration. No other man had ever made her feel that wanton. That wild. But the temptation was there burning deep inside of her like a bullet to see if it would happen again the next time he kissed her. Lifting her chin, she said, "I'll deal with it."

She just had to figure out how.

FIONA GALLAGHER WAS going to be a definite problem for him, D.C. mused. Hadn't he reminded her, while they'd been handling those young punks, that you had to be careful what you wished for? All he'd wanted was a little adventure to relieve his boredom. And fate had served him a double whammy. A mystery surrounding one of the world's most famous diamonds and a woman who stirred his blood just by being there.

Why? He wasn't so much baffled by the question as intrigued. He'd been attracted to beautiful women before. Many pleasurable times. And Fiona certainly was beautiful. The fair skin, the dark hair, the face that might have served as a model for an Italian cameo—and that list was just for starters. Once they'd arrived at the Blue Pepper, she'd slipped out of her coat and he'd gotten a good look at those long legs, the sexy compact body and swimmer's shoulders. A lesser man might have had to stop his tongue from hanging out.

The red dress left as much skin bare as it covered, and it clung in just the right places. In the cramped office where Chance had escorted them so that his man could authenticate the diamond, D.C. had been so close that her arm had brushed his when she'd taken the Rubinov out. His palms had itched with the desire to take her hand and turn her into his arms. The impulse to touch her right there, right then, had been unprofessional and almost overwhelming.

To control it, he'd stuffed his hands in his pockets and sincerely regretted not having given in to the temptation to run his hands over that combination of cool silk and warm skin earlier, when they'd kissed.

Then there was the kiss itself. No other woman had ever pushed the limits of his control that way. D.C. prided himself on being able to handle almost anything life sent him. But Fiona Gallagher was making him rethink that.

There was something about her, something that he was determined to understand. He figured he had time since they were going to be operating as closely together as Siamese twins.

There wasn't a doubt in D.C.'s mind that he and Fiona

would kiss again. And more. One of the things that made a cop a cop was insatiable curiosity. Both of them had it, and both of them would be compelled to discover if lightning could strike more than...twice? Three times?

The possibility had him wishing for a swallow of the cold beer Chance had offered and he'd refused. Instead, he selected a crispy fried shrimp from the plate he'd loaded up from one of the buffet tables.

"So what do you think of Lieutenant Gallagher?"

Chance's tone was casual, but D.C. had been expecting the question ever since Natalie had spirited Fiona off to a nearby table. Before an interrogation, one always separated the subjects. "I think she has good friends who are worried about her. I imagine that your wife is asking Fiona a similar question." D.C. chewed, swallowed and helped himself to another shrimp. Fiona had been right. The food was excellent.

"Natalie's a bit worried about the two of you working together. Fiona doesn't have any family—except for us."

D.C. met Chance's eyes. "None?"

"Her parents died when she was four. She was adopted, but it didn't work out. The only detail she'd ever shared with Natalie was that she was returned to the adoption agency at Christmastime."

D.C. felt a tightening around his heart. "That had to have been tough."

"Yeah. After that, she was in the foster care system until she went into the police academy in Atlanta. She met Natalie at a conference and shortly after that, she asked for a transfer and joined the high-profile crime division up here." Chance paused to take a swallow of his beer. "I told my wife the two of you will mix about as well as oil and water."

D.C. smiled and selected a stuffed mushroom. "An interesting analogy." With enough shaking, oil and water mixed fine—temporarily. "But you're right. I often have more of an out-of-the-box approach to my work than the lieutenant does."

Chance raised both hands, palms out. "I'm not criticizing your style."

D.C. grinned at him. "That would be like the pot calling the kettle black."

"True."

"I think we can work it out." His smile faded. "How good is she?"

"Fiona's the best cop Natalie has."

"Then that's why I need to work with her. You and I both know that hacking into the security system of the National Gallery is either the work of a real pro or a very gifted amateur. Or both. And it's a pretty safe bet that someone inside the gallery has to be involved."

"Agreed. I'd like nothing more than to help you out on this one. Natalie feels the same way. But we may be otherwise engaged at almost any time…"

D.C. studied Fiona's boss. When they'd been working together in Iraq, Chance had had plenty of time to talk about his wife's interesting background. Natalie Gibbs-Mitchell was the daughter of a master thief. And she would have been no slouch herself if she hadn't chosen a career in law enforcement. As it was, Chance claimed he'd never run into anyone who could get into a safe as fast as she could.

Then he shifted his attention to Fiona. "I think the lieutenant and I will make a good team. She's methodical."

"And you're more intuitive and impulsive."

D.C. grinned. "If it makes you feel any better, Fiona has already told me that I'm too bossy. I agreed to work on it."

Chance studied him for a moment. "You might very well

make a good team. Natalie says Fiona has the tenacity of a bulldog. Reminds me a bit of you."

As if Chance's smile was a signal, Natalie and Fiona chose that moment to rise from their table and move toward them. D.C. lifted the plate of food and offered. Natalie selected a shrimp. Fiona shook her head.

"We thought it might be time to share theories," Natalie said.

D.C. selected a stuffed mushroom. "It's just a working hypothesis, but I don't believe Amanda Hemmings or her assailant masterminded this heist. What I saw in the sculpture garden came across as the work of amateurs. I scared that guy off without firing a shot."

Fiona asked Chance, "How much is the diamond insured for?"

"Five hundred million. Mr. Shalnokov upped the policy by one million just before he agreed to the exhibition."

"Is that what it's worth?" D.C. asked.

Chance shrugged. "Two years ago, he tested the waters at Christie's, but withdrew the necklace when it didn't immediately sell. This exhibition at the National Gallery has garnered a lot of publicity. Perhaps it will encourage some offers more in line with his goal."

"D.C. and I have already discussed the possibility that money might be his objective," Fiona began.

"And if he's the mastermind behind the theft," D.C. continued.

"Shalnokov gets to collect the insurance and put the Rubinov back into his private collection," Fiona finished.

"The two of you sound as if you've been working together for years," Chance remarked.

"The display case can only be opened with his voice," D.C. pointed out.

At Chance's surprised look he said, "I visited the museum earlier today with my mom and sister, and I got to talking with one of the guards, Bobby Grant. He obviously felt he could talk to me because he has a son stationed in Iraq."

Chance winced. "So much for the secrecy of the security system. Shalnokov insisted on a voice-activated lock since he wouldn't personally be there to deliver or pick up the diamond. He made a digital recording so that his longtime personal assistant, Dr. Regina Meyers, had to be there to put the diamond in and take it out of the case."

"So all the thieves would have needed was a good digital recording of Shalnokov's voice to unlock the display case?" Fiona asked.

"Correct," Chance said. "I didn't see the point of arguing about it since there was very little likelihood that the other layers of security surrounding the Rubinov would be compromised. As far as Shalnokov being the prime suspect, there are some things you should know. One—he's in a wheelchair and never leaves his home. It's built like a fortress on about a hundred acres of land in Virginia. All the arrangements for the exhibition, including the negotiation for extra insurance, were handled by Regina Meyers. I checked into her. She has Ph.D. in clinical psychology and Shalnokov hired her ten years ago."

"So Shalnokov's right-hand man is also his personal therapist," D.C. said.

"Perhaps," Chance said.

"Lack of mobility doesn't have to be an issue. Again, he wouldn't be working alone—someone inside the museum has to be involved," Fiona said. "Perhaps one or more of the people who escaped in that van. And if he hired the job done, Shalnokov could have provided a recording of his voice."

"But if you're planning on stealing your own necklace, why add a particular bit of security that could come back to bite you?" D.C. asked.

"Good point," Fiona said.

After licking his thumb, D.C. took out his notebook and began to write. "We'll need to find out if Shalnokov has any connection to Amanda Hemmings."

"I'll give you our file on Shalnokov," Chance offered. "And I'll try to arrange a time for you to meet with him. You may have to settle for Regina Meyers."

Fiona glanced at D.C. "Just before Nat and I joined you, I checked with the hospital again. Amanda Hemmings is suffering from a skull fracture and a possible concussion. We won't be able to talk to her until first thing in the morning."

"Afterward, we should talk to General Eddinger," D.C. said. "She'll be able to fill us in on what she knows. Hemmings has been working with her for the past year. I'll set that up."

A cell phone rang, and all four reached for theirs.

"It's my brother." D.C. raised his cell to his ear. "What did you find?" While he listened, he scribbled more notes.

Fiona could see it, the moment that he got something. Everything about him went absolutely still. She felt her pulse give a skip.

"Got it. Thanks."

"What is it?" she asked.

"Private Amanda Hemmings is the great-niece of Arthur Franks."

Chance gave a long, low whistle.

"Good heavens," Natalie said.

"His name was mentioned in the *Washington Post* article about the diamond," Fiona murmured. "Wasn't he rumored to have had something to do with the Rubinov's reappearance ten years ago?"

"Yes," D.C. said. "Nothing was ever proven. According to my brother, Arthur Franks is currently serving ten years at a minimum security prison about an hour away from here in Cumberland, Maryland. And there's more. He has a twenty-year-old grandson who is currently a freshman at American University. Billy Franks's major is Information Technology Studies and he's reputed to be something of a boy genius."

"Looks like our prime suspect list has just lengthened," Fiona said.

D.C. pocketed his notebook and pen and met Fiona's eyes. "Since there's not much we can do about interviewing any of them until the morning, I vote we stay and enjoy the party."

Fiona stared at him. He looked perfectly serious.

"That's a great idea," Natalie said. "There's a live band playing on the patio off the lobby. Chance and I would be dancing if I could move."

D.C. met Fiona's eyes. "Would you care to dance?"

Fiona frowned at D.C. "No."

Natalie beamed a smile at him. "Chance told me I was going to like you."

"C'mon." D.C. held out his hand.

"We can't."

"Speak for yourself. My mother saw to it that both of her sons could find their way around a dance floor. You never learned?"

"Of course. I can dance. But I want to—"

"Go back to your office and work."

Natalie patted D.C.'s arm. "Fiona's an all work and no play kind of girl. It's the way she escapes from an overabundance of Christmas cheer."

Fiona shot Natalie a glare. "I don't think I have to justify wanting to work. Just because we can't talk to suspects tonight doesn't mean that—"

"We can't talk about them, posit some theories, develop a plan of attack," D.C. continued. "We can even come up with a to-do list."

"Exactly."

"And we can do all those things just as easily on the dance floor as we can at your office. At least I can." There was a question and a challenge in his eyes as he snagged her hand.

"I work best when it's quiet."

"And I don't. C'mon, Lieutenant, look at it as an opportunity to get to know your new partner. Sometimes I get my best ideas when I'm concentrating on something else. We can always go back to your office and try it your way later."

"One dance." Fiona let D.C. lead her toward the stairs to the lower level. "But I'm going to figure out how you do that."

"What?" He hooked his cane over his arm and grabbed the rail as they descended.

"Talk me into things I don't want to do."

"It's my charm."

Fiona snorted. She noticed how easily he cut a path for them through the crowd in the lobby. It wasn't just his size, she decided. Nor was it merely the effect of the uniform. The man projected an air of authority that encouraged others to do what he wanted.

When a waitress accidentally jostled them, then quickly apologized, D.C.'s smile had the young woman blushing. On top of the charm, he had a very potent smile.

But neither accounted fully for the intense effect he had on her senses. She'd never experienced anything like it before. Every time he was close, every time she looked into his eyes, she felt as if she were being swept under in a kind of riptide.

And each time it happened, she seemed to have less power to prevent it.

As he drew her onto the dance floor, the band segued into a ballad. D.C.'s grip on her hand remained light, but she was aware that his palms were hard, his fingers calloused. And she couldn't prevent herself from wondering what they would feel like on her skin when he really touched her. He hadn't yet. But she'd wanted him to—desperately.

When he reached the center of the dance floor, she turned to face him. Dancers moved past them, around them, but he didn't take her into his arms, and she didn't step forward.

"It's not going to continue this way. We agreed you're not always going to call the shots," she said.

D.C. brows shot up. "Did I order you to dance?"

"No. But you manipulated me onto the dance floor."

"Okay. I can plead guilty to that. So you can lead if you want."

"I'm not talking just about this." Keeping her eyes steady on his, she said, "One dance. Then we'll go to my office and we'll see which venue allows us to make the most progress."

He smiled. "You're cute when you start spouting procedure."

She was stalling. But she wasn't the only one, Fiona realized. The dancers moved around them, but they remained still. It gave her some satisfaction to know that they both were a bit wary of what they might be getting into. Hell, it was only a dance. She moved first, placing a hand on his shoulder and stepping closer.

D.C. took her other hand, put his free one on the small of her back and guided her into the music. To her surprise, he didn't immediately pull her close. Using only the slightest pressure, he eased her into the rhythm of the music. Still, by the time they'd circled the floor once, every nerve in her body had begun to throb. And when his thigh brushed against hers, the shock of the contact nearly had her stumbling.

"Easy," he murmured.

They were closer now, and the heat that had exploded between them when they'd kissed was building again. She wanted nothing more than to melt into him, to give in to that sense of powerlessness. She'd felt the same way when they were standing shoulder to shoulder in that small office while the gemologist examined the stone. A little flutter of panic steadied her, and she tilted her head back to meet his eyes. "I don't understand what's happening here."

"Do you have to?"

"I like to understand things. It's absolutely ridiculous to think that it has anything to do with that diamond."

As the rhythm of the dance changed, D.C. eased her out so that she could turn in a circle before he drew her back.

"If you don't believe in legends, what do you believe in?"

"Facts."

"Me, too. It's what drew me into the military police. I like to uncover them, examine them and see how they fit together."

"Yes. Exactly. That's why I entered the police academy, too. So you agree that the legend surrounding the Rubinov is ridiculous."

"Not quite. The thing about legends is they often contain an odd mixture of facts and—"

"Fantasies," Fiona insisted. "I prefer just pain facts."

"Okay," D. C. agreed amiably.

The music had slowed again, and Fiona realized that they were standing very close. So close that she could feel his breath on her cheek.

"So, let's talk facts. Fact number one here is that I want you and you want me."

She could hardly deny it. Not when her heart was racing so fast. Not when each cell in her body was yearning.

"And we're going to have to figure out what to do about it."

"I—I have to think."

For an instant, he pulled her closer and she felt the press of his body against hers. This time, if he hadn't been holding her, she would have melted. Then he gently eased her back. "Don't you ever just let loose and enjoy yourself?"

She frowned. "Of course I do."

"When was the last time you did?"

Fiona thought. And thought.

"If you can't remember, it's been too long."

"I'm just taking the time to choose my best example."

"Right."

"Okay. I went to the Lincoln Center two weeks ago and enjoyed myself thoroughly."

"The Importance of Being Earnest?"

She stared at him. "You saw it?"

"It's one of my favorites."

Fiona stared at him. "Mine, too. It's so absurdly ridiculous. I own the DVD."

"With Reese Witherspoon and Judy Dench."

She nodded.

"And they said we had nothing in common."

When he drew her closer, Fiona didn't resist. And for the first time since she'd stepped into his arms, she allowed herself to relax. He was right about one thing. Doing something just for the pure enjoyment of it wasn't a regular part of her life. She couldn't recall the last time she'd danced with a man. When D.C. ran his fingers up her back, she managed not to purr. But she did close her eyes and rest her head against his shoulder.

Just for a moment. But the moment stretched, and Fiona only realized her mistake when she felt the press of bricks against her back. She opened her eyes to find that D.C. had not only steered her off the dance floor, but they were now standing behind the row of Christmas trees that lined the inner wall of the patio. Beyond his shoulder, the tree lights blinked on and off. On and off.

Her heart gave one good kick, then began to race. "If the dance is over, we'd better get to my office."

"First things first." He ran one finger down her throat. "I want to kiss you again."

Fiona stiffened, but it was a thrill that raced through her. "I agreed to a dance, not—"

"You can stop me with a simple no."

But she didn't say it. She might not understand it, but there was no denying that she wanted this. Hadn't she been expecting it all night? Wasn't that the real reason she'd let down her guard on the dance floor? For this...

He didn't move so quickly this time, and it gave her time to anticipate. As his head lowered, heat shimmered from her center to her belly and then to her throat. When his tongue traced her mouth, then slipped between her lips, she gripped his shoulders and hung on. His fingers threaded through her hair, then skimmed over her shoulders, and all the while his mouth barely brushed against hers. It wasn't even a kiss, she thought. Not really. It was more of a promise that she desperately wanted fulfilled.

She heard herself make some small sound. His name? She couldn't make out the word over the pounding of her heart.

Then those hard hands moved slowly down her body, lingering for a long, breathless moment at the sides of her breasts. Even through the thin silk of her dress, she felt the meticulous press of those hard palms, those calloused fingers as they moved lower down her body to grip her hips.

"I want to touch you, Fiona." He didn't wait for permission, but moved in, trapping her between the wall and his body. "I want to really touch you."

She could feel everything—the sharp nip of his teeth on her bottom lip, the scrape of the bricks against her back, the hard planes and angles of his body. But most of all, she felt that clever hand moving from her hip down her thigh. Fire and ice shimmered in its wake.

"I thought of doing this earlier on the street." His hot whispered words feathered along her skin and burned through her mind. "And I can't seem to get it out of my mind."

As he slid his fingers beneath the hem of her dress and began to push the material up her thigh, she began to tremble—one convulsive shudder after another. As if she'd given him a signal, his mouth became harder, hungrier. And those calloused fingers moved higher and higher up her thigh.

When they slipped beneath the edge of her panties and into her heat, she arched back and let the pleasure sear her. She felt a delicious pressure begin to build inside of her, and she let her mind fill with the image of letting him take her right here. Right now.

No, a part of her screamed.

Yes, another part of her urged. And it was that part of her, the part she didn't understand at all that had her digging deep for the strength to say, "No."

D.C.'S HANDS IMMEDIATELY stilled, but it took all of his concentration to withdraw his fingers. To steady himself, he focused on the task of pulling down her dress and discovered his hand was trembling.

No woman had ever made him tremble before.

Because he felt like a diver surfacing from a depth of several hundred feet down, he braced one hand against the brick wall before he eased himself away.

She'd done it again. She'd made him lose control. Even now, the details were coming back in bits and pieces. He'd simply had to touch her. The need to do so had been so compelling that he'd forgotten where they were.

Having risky, semi-public sex with a woman had never been his style. Before.

In the blinking of the tree lights, her skin was flushed, and he could see that her hair was mussed. Her eyes had darkened to the color of finely aged whiskey. He didn't dare look at her mouth or he'd have to taste her again. And all of his brain cells would shut down for the night.

"This is crazy."

Her voice was husky, but she'd found it.

He tried his own. "Yeah."

"We nearly—"

"Yeah."

"We have to do something about this."

"Yeah." He couldn't have agreed more.

"Is that all you can say?" She placed two hands on his chest and shoved.

In spite of the weakness in his knees, he remained erect. But he bit back another *yeah*. Any second now, he was going to get it together.

"Don't tell me you didn't plan this." She straightened her dress and finger-combed her hair. "We have an investigation to work on. All that talk about discussing the case on the dance floor. It was all just a...ruse." She strode past him.

He let her make it to the line of Christmas trees before he said, "What *are* we going to do about this, Fiona?"

She whirled back and met his eyes. "I'll let you know when I decide."

He managed a smile as he moved forward to join her. "Okay. You can take the lead on this one."

5

THE SHRILL SOUND of the alarm had Fiona sitting straight up in bed. Automatically she reached out and slammed her hand on the button to end the noise. Then she peered groggily at the time: 6:30 a.m. She blinked and peered again. It couldn't be. But the scent of coffee told her that the automatic percolator that she'd preset the night before was right in tune with her alarm.

With a groan, she threw the covers back, slid out of bed and headed for the bathroom. The last time she'd checked, the time had been 4:50 a.m. And the blame for the fact that she'd gotten less than two hours of sleep could be laid squarely at the feet of D. C. Campbell.

He'd told her that she could take the lead on deciding the next step in their relationship, and he'd kept his word.

Twisting faucets in her shower, she shed her nightshirt and waited for the first sign of steam. D.C. had been all focused on business as they'd left the restaurant. She had to admire his ability to transition from lover to cop. He was efficient, too. By the time they'd reached their cars, there was no need to stop at her office because they'd managed to agree on a full schedule for the following day. At the top of their list was talking to Amanda Hemmings. They'd meet at the hospital at 8:00 a.m. Then they'd pay a visit to D.C.'s General Eddinger and after that, they'd drop by the National Gallery. That would give Chance time to return the necklace and try to determine how the security system had been breached. Chance was also going to call the Federal Prison at Cumberland. If Amanda had had any contact with her great-uncle, Chance was going to try to get Fiona and D.C. in to interview Arthur Franks.

D.C. had insisted on following her home, but he hadn't seen her to the door. Nor had he touched her again, not even in the most casual of ways. It was only when she'd closed and locked her apartment door behind her that it had sunk in. He really was going to let her take the lead.

She'd spent most of the night mulling over her options. But now, at least, she'd made up her mind.

Stepping under the spray, she poured shower gel into her hand, lathered lavishly, then reached for shampoo. As water sluiced over her, she reviewed the decision she'd reached. She'd always prided herself on being a practical woman. And she'd come to a reasonable and logical solution to the overwhelming attraction she felt for D.C.

She was going to give in to it. It wasn't that big a deal, really. After all, she'd nearly given in to it last night at the Blue Pepper.

She turned the faucets off and then pressed a hand against the nerves jumping in her stomach. Usually, when she made a decision, that was it. She didn't have second thoughts or feel the need to rethink it over and over.

Nor had she ever before wondered if the decision had been hers to make—or if it had been ripped away from her the moment she'd first seen him standing on the other side of the Rubinov diamond.

No. She was not going to entertain that possibility. She was going to stick to the facts. Grabbing a towel, she wrapped it around her hair, then used another one to dry off. Number one, they were mutually attracted to one another. Two, trying to ignore what they were feeling was…distracting and might interfere with their investigation.

And ignoring the attraction might turn out to be impossible in any case, nagged a little voice at the back of her mind.

Fiona firmly pushed aside the thought. As it was, the chemistry between them was so volatile, it might burn out right after they had sex. Problem solved. And if it didn't…?

The nerves in her stomach did another annoying little jig. Grabbing a robe from the hook over the door, Fiona ran fingers through her still-damp hair as she headed for her small galley kitchen.

She poured a cup of the freshly brewed coffee and blew on the hot liquid as she strode back into her bedroom. She'd made her decision. Taking a fortifying sip, she selected clothes, then began the next phase of her morning routine— blow-drying her hair.

The pounding on her door began just as Fiona was fastening a gold hoop in her ear. Who…? The tightening in her gut answered her question before she even released the deadbolt and opened the door to the length of the security chain.

D.C. grinned at her through the crack. "Good. I see you're up and ready."

"What are you doing here?" She shot back the chain and opened the door. He was wearing black denim jeans, a turtleneck and a black leather jacket. He nearly filled the doorway.

And he was going to be hers. As the decision solidified inside of her, some of her nerves settled. Others started a little jig. To cover them, she said, "I thought we were supposed to meet at the hospital."

"I figured it would be more efficient if we went in the same car. Safer, too. There's about four inches of snow out there, and I've got four-wheel drive. You don't. Besides, traveling together will allow us to discuss what we've learned, strategize. I figured it will save us time. Am I right?"

"Yes."

He smiled then. "But it's your call."

"Okay. We'll go in your car."

"Good." D.C. noted the hint of nerves in her eyes as he moved past her, and they settled some of his own. "Got any coffee?"

"Help yourself."

After he spotted the half-full pot, he kept his back to her as he searched her cupboards and located a mug. The simplicity of using one car and the fact that they'd soon be dealing with the media had been two of the reasons he'd given himself for driving over instead of meeting her at the hospital.

The most comfortable ones.

The one that caused him the most concern was that he'd awakened with an inexplicable need to see her. Why? The *n* word bothered him a bit, but not enough to dampen his curiosity.

The other reason he'd come here this morning was that he didn't want to give her too much time to decide whether or not they were going to become lovers. And he was prepared to influence her decision if he had to.

He found sugar in the third cupboard he opened. Then he located milk in the refrigerator. She kept a tidy kitchen, but he found absolutely nothing edible to go with the coffee.

Turning around, he leaned a hip against the counter. "What do you usually do for breakfast?"

"I pick it up on the way to the station."

She'd remained standing against the door she'd closed behind him. They were both keeping their distance. Sipping coffee, he studied her in the first rays of sunlight pouring through the window.

Gone was the red dress, but she still looked like a fashion

plate. The dove-gray jacket and slacks were neatly tailored. The killer shoes had been replaced by practical low-heeled boots. The result was neat and professional. Today, the only hint of the passion he'd discovered beneath that cool surface was the bold purple color of her blouse.

He sipped coffee again, then set his mug down. "I also wanted to find out what you've decided about us. We'll be busy once we get to the hospital."

Her brows rose. "I didn't know there was a deadline."

"I figured you'd want to get everything settled so we can concentrate on the case." He saw annoyance and then agreement flash into her eyes.

He wanted it settled, too. Being attracted to a woman, making love to a woman, should be simple. It always had been before, but D.C.'s instinct had warned him from the first that whatever happened with Fiona would be complicated. And that was all right. Hadn't he always preferred life when it promised a little adventure?

"All right." She moved forward a few steps. "I've given it careful thought, and I've decided I don't want to fight this attraction any longer."

D.C. felt his heart give a little kick, and he was glad that he'd set down the mug.

She whirled, paced a few steps, then turned to face him. "It's the logical choice."

"You won't get an argument from me, Fiona." When he took a step toward her, she held up a hand.

"Let me finish. We're adults, we want each other and we're going to be working together for a while. We're both smart and good at what we do, so we should be able to keep things compartmentalized."

"Things?"

She waved a hand impatiently. "You and me having sex and finding out who stole the Rubinov from the National Gallery."

He studied her. "Why is it so important to keep the two things separate?"

She stuffed her hands in her pockets. "Because the diamond's legend thing could muddy things up. I don't want either of us to get hurt."

D.C. thought of what Chance had told him about her, of how young she'd been when she'd lost her parents and then her adoptive family.

She met his eyes steadily. "I'm willing to go forward with this as long as we set up some parameters."

"Such as?"

"I prefer to keep things tidy and predictable. So I'd like us to agree that we'll enjoy each other temporarily."

"Temporarily meaning?"

"For the length of time we're working together. And then we'll go our separate ways. No harm. No hassles. No foul."

He moved toward her then. It gave him some satisfaction to see her stiffen slightly. But she didn't back up. "I'm not much good at tidy and predictable. Will that be a deal breaker?"

She frowned. "I don't want either one of us to get hurt."

"I won't hurt you, Fiona." He touched just the ends of her hair. "I can agree with that part."

"You won't hurt me on purpose," she said.

Anger surged at the realization that someone *had* hurt her. Intentionally. He wanted to ask who. And he wanted badly to pay them back. Another part of him wanted even more to scoop her up, carry her into the bedroom and make her forget the hurt.

But that wasn't what she needed. So instead, he leaned down and gently touched his mouth to hers. Then he stepped back, grabbed her coat off a nearby chair and held it for her.

"Now that we've settled everything, let's go to the hospital."

"We haven't settled anything yet."

"Sure we have—unless you want to modify our to-do list. Ever since I walked in, I've been wondering how long it might take me to get you out of that neat little suit. If we stay here any longer, we're going to find out."

Without a word, she snatched her coat and led the way out the door.

SEVEN-THIRTY WAS A BUSY TIME on a hospital floor. Staff wheeled carts filled with breakfast trays down the corridors. New patients were being admitted and escorted to rooms. Using a combination of D.C.'s charm and Fiona's badge, they quickly made it past the floor nurse. Since the doctor hadn't made his rounds yet, the nurse wasn't able to update them on Amanda's condition.

According to the uniformed officer sitting at Private Hemmings's door, they were her first visitors. It was a small, private room, and Amanda Hemmings, her eyes closed, her head swathed in bandages, looked very young and defenseless lying in the bed.

There were blue shadows beneath Amanda's eyes, a tube in her nose and an IV feeding into a vein on one of her hands. Ignoring a tug of sympathy, Fiona noted that her breakfast sat untouched on a nearby table.

On the ride over, D.C. had filled her in on more details that his brother had discovered about Amanda's background. Not that there were very many. She was twenty years old. She'd lost both of her parents, her dad when she was ten and her mom two years later. When her uncle, Billy's father, had refused to take her in, she'd slipped into the foster care system. She'd joined the army right out of high school. Fiona couldn't help but note how similar their stories were. Amanda Hemmings had chosen the military as her safety net while Fiona had joined the police academy.

Still, regardless of how similar their stories were, she had to be objective. Amanda Hemmings was the great-niece of the kind of thief who could have set up the attempted snatch of the Rubinov. Until they found out for sure if Amanda had been in contact with Arthur Franks, the innocent-looking private was looking pretty guilty.

She and D.C. had decided in the car that he would question Amanda. Since he'd met her a few times in General Eddinger's office, she'd probably be more at ease with him. In other words, Fiona was to play bad cop. Usually, she relished the role.

Very deliberately, she moved to the foot of the bed and shifted her gaze to D.C. He was studying Hemmings also, and once again, he seemed to fill the space. It was more than his size and more than his aura of command. For her, the man was different. She'd only had to see him filling her doorway this morning to know that she'd made the only decision that she could.

Sex had always been pleasurable. But when she thought about making love to D.C., touching him, being touched by him, pleasure shot right into the pain zone.

Getting out of her apartment had been a struggle. From the moment she'd seen him through the crack in the door, she'd wanted him. It had taken all of her concentration to lay out the ground rules. When he'd talked about how quickly they could be in bed together, her knees had gone weak.

What would happen when they really did make love? She'd very nearly found out. When she'd grabbed her coat from him, she'd very nearly tossed it on the floor and jumped him.

And that wasn't like her at all.

Perhaps she should have. The idea of it thrilled her. Perhaps that was the only way to put an end to this aching need inside of her.

"Amanda, can you hear me?"

Ruthlessly, Fiona forced her mind back to the job.

Amanda's eyes fluttered open. Gradually, her initial disorientation faded and her gaze became fixed on D.C.

He covered one of her hands with his. "I'm Captain D. C. Campbell. I run the military police unit at Fort McNair. General Eddinger introduced us once."

For a moment, she studied D.C. "I don't…remember."

"That's all right."

"No. No, it's not."

There was confusion in her voice, but it was the hint of panic that caught Fiona's full attention.

D.C. smiled warmly at her. "I'm here with Lieutenant Gallagher to ask you about what happened last night in the sculpture garden."

Amanda moistened her lips. "Sculpture garden…?"

"Right next to the National Gallery. You were at the National Mall distributing brochures for a toy drive to benefit the families of vets who are recuperating at Walter Reed. Do you remember that?"

There was a stretch of silence as she closed her eyes. When she opened them again, she turned her hand and gripped D.C.'s like a lifeline. "No. I'm sorry."

"It's all right." D.C.'s tone was gentle as he eased himself onto the edge of the bed. "Maybe you remember visiting one of the exhibits at the gallery. There's a new one featuring a legendary diamond. The Rubinov has received quite a bit of attention from the press."

"A diamond?"

"A big one. And it's blue."

"No. I…can't… I—"

"Don't try. Instead, why don't you tell me what you do remember? Take your time."

She drew in a deep breath. "I remember waking up a while ago. There was a woman next to my bed, and she told me I was in a hospital and I was going to be fine. Then I fell asleep again."

"You don't remember anything before that?"

"No…no. Who am I?"

"You're Amanda Hemmings."

Fiona kept her gaze fixed on the young woman while D.C. filled her in on what he knew, save for the part about finding the Rubinov diamond in her pocket. It was a very convenient time to have amnesia. Faking it would buy both Amanda and her accomplices time. But something deep in Fiona's gut told her that what she was witnessing wasn't a performance.

When D.C. had finished his summary of Amanda's work history at Fort McNair, she asked, "Why can't I remember?"

"You suffered a blow to the head. Your skull was fractured and you may have a concussion. The memory loss is probably temporary." He slipped his hand from hers, took out a card, and put it on the stand next to the bed. "Just get some rest, and I'm betting you'll start remembering things shortly. When you do, I want you to give me a call. Will you do that?"

"Yes."

"Good. Lieutenant Gallagher and I are going to let your doctor know that you're having some memory problems. He'll be able to explain it better to you than I can. We'll check in with you later today."

Together they moved out of the room. D.C. waited until the door swung shut behind them before he said, "I believe her."

Fiona sighed. "Look at the evidence. She had the Rubinov in her pocket. Her great-uncle could have planned the job from behind bars and she could have been involved in carrying it out."

"We don't know she had any contact with him."

"We'll have that information soon. Faking amnesia buys her time. It buys her accomplices time, too."

D.C. grinned at her as they stopped at the nurse's station. "You believe her, too."

"It doesn't matter what I believe. She has to be involved somehow. She knows something."

"Agreed."

"As soon as we get out of this no-cell-phone area, I'm going to check in with Natalie."

"Good move." D.C. turned to smile at the nurse and fill her in on Amanda's condition. Then he took Fiona's arm and led her to the elevator. "Now we'll see what my general has to say about Amanda Hemmings."

FIONA WAS STILL ON THE PHONE with Natalie and scribbling busily in her notebook when D.C. spotted a popular coffee and donut chain. He swung his car into the drive-through line and rolled down his window.

The one piece of news she'd conveyed to him so far was that Amanda had indeed paid a visit to her great-uncle at the Cumberland Federal Prison sometime in mid-October. Chance would have more details later.

"Okay, thanks." Fiona paused to tap her pencil on the notepad. "Good luck."

He wasn't picking up much information from her end of the conversation. When the voice came through the speaker asking him to place his order, D.C. said, "Six of your blueberry scones and a half dozen assorted donuts."

He turned to Fiona just as she was filing her notebook and her cell into her purse. "What's your pleasure?"

For a moment, her eyes met his and as their gazes held, the temperature in the car seemed to rise by several degrees.

"Sorry for the Freudian slip," he said. "But I can't seem to get the idea of touching you out of my mind."

Even when he'd been questioning Amanda Hemmings, he'd been very aware of Fiona standing at the foot of the bed. He'd caught that fresh floral scent she wore even above the antiseptic smell of the hospital.

Fiona took a deep breath and then let it out. Her gaze never wavered. "Are you always this blunt?"

"Will there be anything else, sir?"

"Yes," D.C. murmured. But he didn't turn back to the speaker. Instead, he gripped Fiona's chin and with his other hand, he skimmed fingers along her throat to where a pulse was fluttering wildly. It had been a long time since he'd had that second taste of her in the Blue Pepper. Too long.

He drew her mouth slowly to his. "Just a taste." But his intentions faded the moment their lips met and then held. Her flavors went straight to his head...there were so many more than he remembered. The initial sweetness, the spicy heat and a surprising tartness that his system absorbed like a punch in the gut.

God, how had he been able to wait so long for this? How had he managed to get out of her apartment without having her? Changing the angle of the kiss, he plunged them both deeper. Heat flashed to fire in an instant and what he tasted now was a mix of need and ripe surrender. Was it hers? His? Or something they created together?

Fiona couldn't think clearly. His mouth was so...demanding. So hot, so greedy. His teeth nipped, nibbled; his tongue tangled with hers. No one had ever kissed her like this—as if he had all the time in the world and intended to take it. She felt herself slipping into that place that only D.C. had ever taken her to—a place where only the two of them existed.

In some far off corner of her mind, she knew where they were. The air slipping in through the open window was sharp with the sting of winter and carried the scent of coffee and exhaust fumes. She should pull back. But she simply couldn't stop kissing D.C. He touched. She wanted. It was that simple. That compelling.

Not even the skip of fear was enough to keep her from framing his face with her hands. She absorbed the sharp line of his cheekbone, the strength of his jaw. Then she ran her hands down the hard muscles of his chest. Someone moaned. Even as the sound died away, she tried to get closer. She had to get closer. Unsnapping her seat belt, she started to crawl across the console that separated them.

It was the sharp blast of a horn that finally penetrated her conscious mind. But it was D.C.'s hands on her shoulders that stopped her and settled her back in her seat. For just a moment, he rested his forehead on hers. The sound of his ragged breathing filled the car. "Sorry. We have to postpone this for a while."

"Good grief," she murmured as reality finally penetrated. "I nearly…"

"Yes, you did. And I wouldn't have done a thing to stop you. Although the backseat might have provided more space."

A brilliant image flashed into her mind of lying on the backseat with D.C. Naked. Limbs intertwined, moving as one.

The horn started up again—several impatient, staccato beeps. Releasing her, D.C. turned and waved a hand at the driver of the car behind them. "There just aren't enough places in Washington private enough for car sex."

Her head was still swimming a bit, but she managed to

raise a brow. "And I suppose car sex is a regular part of your repertoire?" It had very nearly become a part of hers.

He chuckled. "Not recently. But I'm sure I haven't forgotten the basics."

A little disconcerted that the thought was so appealing, she said, "We have a job to do."

"Agreed."

"So no more kissing until we get through our to-do list."

He snagged her hand and raised it to his lips. "A practical idea, but I'm not sure it will work. I'm thinking I made a strategic blunder when I didn't follow my instincts at your apartment. We could go back."

The warmth flowing up her arm almost had Fiona agreeing. What in the world was wrong with her? She was a sensible woman. At least she always had been. "I don't imagine your general likes to be kept waiting."

D.C. sighed. "There's that."

"Sir, if your order is complete, you can drive up to the next window." Even through the tinny sounding speaker, the voice was annoyed.

"Coffee?" he asked Fiona.

"Small. Black."

"And to eat?"

"Nothing."

D.C. turned, ordered two coffees, and then pulled up to the payment window. "I thought you said you stopped on the way to work to pick up breakfast."

"I do when I'm hungry."

D.C. passed her a coffee, waited until she'd secured it in the cup holder, then handed her the box of donuts. "Humor me and try one of the blueberry scones. We have a long day ahead of us."

She narrowed her eyes. "Are you going to keep nagging until I eat something?"

He grinned at her. "Guaranteed. The scones are General Eddinger's favorites."

"Bribing your boss?" Fiona asked. But she broke off half a scone before she passed the box back to him.

"Just smoothing the waters a bit." He selected a donut, then shifted the box carefully to the backseat. "My impression is that General Eddinger likes Amanda very much. She's not going to be pleased with the way things are shaping up."

He pulled out into traffic. "The last thing you said to your captain was 'good luck.' Why does she need it?"

Fiona wrinkled her nose. "The commissioner is insisting that she hold a news conference to announce the attempted theft of the Rubinov. Chance has informed both the gallery and Shalnokov, so the story could leak any moment. She's going to announce that the investigation is being headed up by me. She's not going to mention the army's involvement."

"Shoot. There goes my five minutes of fame."

Fiona shot him a look. "If she were to mention the fact that we're…collaborating, she'd have to explain why. This way she can keep Amanda Hemmings's name out of it for now. I wonder how much your general had to do with the decision."

"Does it matter?" D.C. asked before he took a long drink of his coffee.

When Fiona didn't answer, he continued, "Has Chance had time to figure out how the security was breached?"

"He's working on it. But he did have some interesting news. When he visited the gallery bright and early this morning, he found a very good copy of the Rubinov in the display case."

D.C. gave a long, low whistle. "So the thieves made a

switch. That throws a whole new light on things. We're definitely not dealing with amateurs here. A good replica would be hard to come by."

"Arthur Franks would know people who could make something like that."

"True. And if everything had gone smoothly, who knows when the robbery would have been discovered?"

"Yeah. By the way, Natalie's just as suspicious as I am about Amanda Hemmings's amnesia story. It's so…convenient. One of our techs got the information off Hemmings's cell phone. She doesn't use it much, but in the last two months, in addition to one phone call to the Cumberland Federal prison, she's called her cousin Billy Franks three times."

"Jase says Billy's reputed to have a real gift with computer systems. I'd like to find out just how good he might be at hacking."

"Right. Natalie gave me an address on him. But I didn't add him to our to-do list because I couldn't figure out a way to pay him a visit without revealing what we know about Amanda."

"That may be a moot point by this afternoon. There's no telling how long we can keep her name out of it."

Fiona bit into a scone, then plucked a fallen crumb off of her lap. "Hemmings made a number of other calls to Fort McNair."

D.C. swung the car into the gate at Fort McNair and grabbed another donut while he waited to be waved on. "What else did you get from Natalie?"

"The warrant came through to search Hemmings's apartment. She's sending it to the two uniforms we have stationed out front and they're going to wait for us."

D.C. pulled into a parking slot. "I vote we go there before we visit the museum."

"I agree."

He grinned at her. "See. I'm trying not to take charge of the investigation."

"Yes, but what if I'd voted to go to the museum first?"

"Then I would have had to persuade you." D.C. slid out of the car, grabbed the donut box and his cane, then joined Fiona on the passenger side. "Let's see what light the General can throw on this case."

6

GENERAL MYRA EDDINGER wasn't at all what Fiona had expected. She was medium height and plump with a round, finely lined face and curly red hair just long enough to tuck behind her ears. From the brief search she'd done on her laptop the night before, Fiona knew that Eddinger was married to a doctor stationed at Walter Reed, and she had two grown sons.

Her handshake was warm, and her smile brightened the moment she spotted the box D.C. carried. She winked at Fiona. "Captain Campbell knows the key to my heart."

Taking the box, she placed it on a small credenza near her desk, then turned up the volume on a small flat-screen TV. "You might want to see this."

Captain Natalie Gibbs-Mitchell was standing in front of a podium speaking into a bank of microphones. The commissioner stood to her right and Chance stood to her left. When the camera went wide, Fiona caught a glimpse of another woman next to Chance. She was tall and striking with just a touch of gray in her hair.

Fiona had seen Natalie face the press before and she was just as admirable now. Her report was concise. There had been an unsuccessful attempt to steal the Rubinov diamond from its display at the National Gallery, but the necklace had been recovered. Then Natalie introduced the woman to Chance's left as Dr. Regina Meyers.

"So that's the woman who's been Gregory Shalnokov's spokesperson for the past ten years," Fiona murmured.

"Yes," Myra Eddinger said. "She's good at her job. The news clip has been running for the past hour, and she's assuring the public that the exhibition will remain open as scheduled until the twenty-third. There ought to be record crowds after this."

Fiona saw an image of her own face flash on the screen, as Natalie identified her as heading up the investigation.

When the news channel switched to another story, General Eddinger clicked off the TV and waved them into chairs at a small conference table. Her expression sobered as she sat down across from them and folded her hands on the desk. "How is Amanda? All I can get from the station nurse is that X-rays and a CAT scan show she has a skull fracture and a probable concussion, but she's in stable condition."

D.C. brought his general up-to-date on Hemmings's condition.

"Amnesia." General Eddinger drew the word out as if she were considering it. Then with a frown, she began to tap the fingers of one hand on the table. "I'll have my husband contact a specialist."

"She could be faking it," Fiona said.

Slowly the general shook her head. "I've known Amanda Hemmings for a year now, and from my observation, she doesn't have a deceitful bone in her body. You're going to find that even though she was found with the Rubinov diamond on her, she's innocent."

"How can you be so sure?" Fiona asked.

The general sighed. "Partly, I'm relying on instinct. The

rest comes from my knowledge of people. I imagine as a cop, you depend on both of those."

"I do."

"Well, I can only hope that neither is failing me in this case. Amanda comes from a very sheltered background. Her father was a conservative Christian. He died when she was ten, and after that, her mother worked two jobs to keep Amanda in a private faith-based school. When her mother died, the authorities contacted an uncle. But evidently Amanda's father had insisted his wife make a complete break with her former family, and the uncle refused to take her in."

"How did Amanda end up in the army?" D.C. asked.

"As soon as she graduated, Amanda enlisted. She felt it was her best way to get a college education. She's very focused, very concerned about living a good Christian life."

The general turned to Fiona. "That's why she contacted you about your toy drive."

"You knew about that?" Fiona asked.

"She asked my opinion." Eddinger folded her hands again. "I'll be honest with you. During the past year, Amanda and I have grown rather close. She's become more than my administrative assistant. My husband and I have had her to our home for dinner frequently. We've invited her to Christmas dinner. I just can't see her involved in something like this."

"Do you know anything about her friends, who she spends time with after hours?"

"I know she's been in contact with a cousin of hers, Billy Franks. He's evidently a technical wunderkind. He's even sold some of the software he's created. She's so proud of him. She brought him here once to give him a tour."

"What's your impression of Billy?" D.C. asked.

Eddinger tilted her head to one side. "Shy and smart. I think the best term to describe him is *geek*. He's of medium height, slender, wears his hair longish and has glasses. As I understand it, she hadn't seen him for years because of her father's split with her mother's family. I think she had some idea of healing old wounds."

"Did you know that Amanda's great-uncle and Billy's grandfather is Arthur Franks, a master thief who's currently incarcerated at the federal prison in Cumberland, Maryland?"

D.C.'s question had Eddinger's eyes widening.

"No. I didn't know that." Rising, she walked to the window and stared out at the grounds. "It casts everything in a slightly different light, doesn't it?"

For a few moments, the silence grew in the room. Then Eddinger turned back to face them. "I still can't believe Amanda is involved in robbing the National Gallery."

Fiona couldn't help but note that the general no longer sounded so convinced of Amanda's innocence.

AMANDA HEMMINGS'S LANDLADY, Claire Ridgeway, let them into the small foyer of one of the row houses that were plentiful in the area of Washington near the Capitol. She was tall, thin, and wore her white hair in a long braid down her back. D.C. guessed her to be in her early sixties. When Fiona handed her the search warrant, she put on a pair of glasses and perused it carefully.

"Is Ms. Hemmings in trouble? Is that why the patrol car has been parked in front of my house all night?"

"She was the victim of a mugging on the National Mall and we're investigating," Fiona said.

"Is she all right?"

Noting the concern in the older woman's eyes, D.C.

said, "She's in stable condition, and she's expected to make a full recovery."

"Good." But the woman let out a sigh as she led them down a flight of stairs to the basement. "Terrible thing. When young people go into the military, your biggest fear is that they'll lose their lives in some faraway country. And then they get injured at home."

"I'm curious." D.C. hitched his cane over one arm and used the wall for support as they descended. "This is a pretty high-rent district. How did Hemmings manage it on a private's pay?"

Claire Ridgeway opened the door before turning to face him. "I own this house. I lost a son in the Gulf War, so I regularly rent this apartment out to one of the enlisted men or women stationed at Fort McNair. I make sure the rent is affordable."

"Do you know Private Hemmings very well?" Fiona asked as Ridgeway led them into the apartment.

"No, not well at all. I interviewed her when I first showed her the place and checked her references. We talked in passing, of course. But we're both busy. I give private violin lessons in the afternoons and early evenings. And when Amanda was home, she kept to herself."

"Did she ever have visitors?" D.C. asked.

The woman frowned thoughtfully. "She brought a young man here once. A few weeks ago. He wasn't military. The clothes were wrong. So was the way he carried himself. I remember thinking that they made an odd sort of couple."

"Can you describe him?" D.C. asked.

"He was of medium height and thin, with longish dark hair and glasses. He wore black jeans and a black leather jacket."

"Thank you, Mrs. Ridgeway," Fiona said. Reaching into her purse, she pulled out a card and handed it to the woman. "If you think of anything else, please don't hesitate to call."

The woman had pulled the door nearly shut when she stopped and turned back to them. "There was something else odd that happened last night. I was letting one of my students out around six o'clock and there was a van parked across the street. It was dark, but they were parked near the streetlight. There were three of them in the vehicle."

"Did you get a good look at any of them?" D.C. asked.

Claire Ridgeway shook her head. "No."

"Do you know how long the van was there?" Fiona asked.

"I can't say exactly. It was gone when I noticed the patrol car."

Fiona thanked the woman again and they moved into the apartment. The moment the door closed behind Ridgeway, Fiona said, "They knew where she lived and they came here to wait for her. That strengthens the theory that Hemmings, her assailant and the other two in the van were working together."

D.C. nodded. "Working together or not, the trio knew she still had the diamond—and they weren't sure how badly she'd been hurt."

"So they came here to cover their bases, hoping that she might still show up with it. Then they scattered when the police showed up."

"That's one theory. It's an interesting case. Parts of the heist argue for a professional, and other parts indicate easily panicked amateurs."

Fiona glanced around the apartment. It was a tiny, one-room space with a counter at one end. Behind it was a kitchen no bigger than an airplane galley. Halfway up one wall was a three-sided bay window that opened at ground level and offered a view of the street.

On another wall was a marble-framed fireplace with a raised hearth. The furnishings were sparse, but each piece looked as if it had been selected carefully. This would have been the first place that belonged to Amanda Hemmings after she left the foster care system. Fiona recalled how careful she'd been about furnishing her first place.

A Victorian-inspired sofa and a carved wooden coffee table filled most of the room. D.C. brushed up against the fireplace as he navigated around them toward the kitchen. She moved toward the desk. Its surface, like the mantle and coffee table, was clutter free. Not even a stray magazine marred the tidiness. In the first drawer she opened, she found a small stack of the brochures advertising the toy drive. Beneath them was a guide book to Washington and the surrounding areas and a Bible that looked as if it was read regularly. Amanda had used one of the brochures to bookmark the guide book at a map of the Smithsonian museums. In another drawer, there were files containing bills, monthly bank statements, a checkbook.

"There's nothing in the freezer or the fridge but some leftover Chinese takeout," D.C. said from behind her. "And her cupboards are nearly as bare as yours."

"This is her first place, the first time she's really been on her own. She probably eats at the base and picks up something on her way home."

It was only as she shut the file drawer that she noticed the tab of a file folder tucked beneath the desk blotter. "Got something," she said as she slipped it out. Carrying it with her, she moved to the sofa and opened it on the coffee table. "It's a bunch of press clippings about the Rubinov."

When D.C. joined her, the legs of the sofa creaked ominously. Ignoring the sound, he helped her arrange the clippings on the coffee table.

For a moment, neither one of them spoke. Something tightened around Fiona's heart. "I'm no expert, but I'd say she was fascinated by the diamond."

"I agree." D.C. tapped a finger on one of the articles. "This one is from the original announcement in October."

Fiona studied the picture and recognized one of the two women. "That's Regina Meyers." In the caption below the photo, the other woman was identified as Charity Watkins, the exhibit's director at the National Gallery.

When her cell rang, Fiona checked the caller ID. "It's Natalie." Then she pressed the speaker phone button so that D.C. could hear.

"Chance has talked with the security people at the National Gallery. Turns out there was a slight problem with the security system yesterday afternoon at five, just as the exhibit closed down. There's evidently a set routine. The guards get everyone out. Then at five, they lock the doors. That's when the infrared security beams go on. Yesterday, at five, the surveillance screens in the security room went blank for about two to three minutes. No alarm sounded, and when they rebooted the system, everything was fine. The diamond was right there in its case. This morning, at Chance's request, they checked the tapes from the cameras in the room and in the hallway that runs behind it, but there's nothing but a blank screen during the crucial three minutes."

"So someone jammed the entire system, including the cameras, for three minutes while they made the switch," D.C. said.

"That's what Chance believes. He figures they went in through a service door at the back of the room."

"Would they have still needed a recording of Shalnokov's voice?" Fiona asked.

"Chance says yes. But a good digital recording would do. And since Shalnokov has never personally visited the exhibit, that's likely."

Fiona glanced down at the newspaper photo. "Dr. Regina Meyers would have one of those."

"Yes, she would. Chance has run another background check on her, and she's clean. She's been with Shalnokov for ten years, ever since he acquired the Rubinov. If she wanted to steal it, she would have had many opportunities. I spoke with her before the news conference. She was intensely grateful for the fact that the robbery was prevented. Any updates on your end?"

"We're in Amanda Hemmings's apartment, and we've found a file of press clippings—a collection of everything that's been printed on the exhibit to date. It looks as if she was fixated on the necklace," Fiona said.

"Good work," Natalie said. "Keep in touch." Then she disconnected.

Neither D.C. nor Fiona spoke for a moment. Then Fiona said, "I'm sitting here trying to convince myself that Amanda might not have been the only one who collected articles on the Rubinov."

"She probably wasn't. The stone seems to fascinate a lot of people."

"Right. But this file can also be read as more evidence that she was involved in the robbery. And I'm trying to view it in a way that makes her look innocent."

D.C. began to gather up the clippings. "First of all, this file is just another piece of evidence. Did you ever do any connect-the-dots puzzles when you were a kid, Fiona?"

She met his eyes. "Yes. But what does that have to do with anything?"

"When I'm investigating a case, I think of it in terms of that kind of a puzzle. But a jigsaw puzzle would work equally well as an analogy. We don't have all the dots or all the pieces yet."

"We've got a lot of them—the necklace in her pocket, a visit to her master thief great-uncle and the clippings."

He covered her hand with his. "These clippings aren't what's bothering you."

Fiona turned to meet his eyes. "I'm having trouble being objective. I want to be on Amanda's side. I keep thinking of the way she looked lying there on the ground last night. And the way she looked in the hospital. And…it's interfering."

"You're bothered because you can't quite keep your personal feelings compartmentalized."

"Exactly." She could hear the frustration in her voice and struggled to control it. "Usually, I can. I do."

"Caring doesn't make you less of a cop. What does your gut tell you about Amanda Hemmings?"

"That's exactly what Natalie asked me last night. I told her I needed more information."

"And now you've got more."

"No matter how damning the evidence is, my gut still tells me that there's some explanation—that she's innocent."

"Why are you questioning your instincts?"

The matter-of-fact way he was asking the questions was calming her. Letting her gaze sweep the room, she gathered her thoughts. "I'm identifying too much with her. Both of us lost our parents at a young age and grew up in the system."

"And survived it."

"We're alike in other ways, too. I saw the police academy as my path to independence. I'm betting Amanda saw joining the armed service in the same light. I walk in here and I see the first place I moved into once I was on my own. My apartment was even smaller than this. I know how much time she spent picking out the desk and the table."

The sofa creaked again.

"And this totally impractical sofa. The one I chose was a love seat. The frame was carved cherry, and I bought it at an antique shop." She ran a hand over the arm. "It was of better quality—but absolute hell to sleep on. And there's no Christmas tree. In fact, there are no holiday decorations at all."

"Christmases in foster care have to be tough."

She turned to face him, and found herself staring into those gray eyes that saw so much. When he took her hand, linked his fingers with hers, feelings sprang to life inside of her again. Sharp, insistent. She couldn't name them, couldn't even begin to understand them. All she could be certain of was that they didn't have to do with Amanda Hemmings or the case. This time, it was D. C. Campbell who had triggered the flood of emotions.

She wasn't a woman who lied to herself. There was no way to deny that the connection between them went beyond the physical. This close, his eyes were a pale gray—the color of thick, impenetrable fog. And she was getting lost in them.

But she didn't step back, didn't move at all. Because once again, she simply couldn't. Something about him was pulling her out of herself, and she was powerless to resist.

In the quiet of the room, she could hear each breath he took in and exhaled. The sound—just the sound—had desire erupting and racing through her in a torrent of heat. Desire and passion—those feelings she could understand. She welcomed them.

She couldn't deny that she wanted him. Desperately. Neither of them moved, but Fiona saw his eyes darken, and she knew that his feelings were marching right along with hers. For the first time, she became aware that his thigh was touching hers, and the room, though it was tiny, seemed suddenly smaller, the air thinner. Her awareness of everything intensified. Her pulse hammering at the base of her throat, his scent, unrepentantly male, filling her each time she breathed.

And his hands. Each one of the fingers linked with hers was like a brand on her skin. He might as well have been touching her everywhere. At the thought, greed, raw and unmanageable, burst to life inside of her. She wanted him to touch her.

She swallowed. "Then there's you. How can I think straight about the case when I want you this much?"

"The problem is mutual. It's high time we solved it."

She wasn't sure who moved first, just that their mouths finally touched and molded. Reason vanished, and Fiona felt herself lost in exploring the shape of his lips, the texture of his tongue moving over hers, and his taste—dark and addictive. It would always be this way with him. Only with him.

When he drew away, she dug the fingers of her free hand into his shoulder and she would have cried out if he hadn't covered her mouth with his fingers.

"Mrs. Ridgeway can't be far."

Mrs. Ridgeway. Even as the reality of where they were came flooding back, Fiona knew she didn't care. What in the world had happened to the practical, sensible woman she used to be? She gripped his hand more tightly. "I want you now."

"Not here."

"I thought you were supposed to be the impulsive one."

"Working on it." He took both of her hands and drew her to her feet.

Fiona expected him to move to the door, but instead he guided her around the coffee table to the fireplace. Then he leaned his cane against the marble and gripped her by the hips. Fiona experienced an instant of disorientation when he lifted her onto the hearth. Then they were eye to eye.

"Yes, this might work," D.C. said. "Game to give it a shot?"

Fiona blinked even as her pulse rocketed and her knees went weak. "I thought you said 'not here.'"

He jerked his head. "I meant not over there on that sofa. We'd make kindling out of it." Turning slightly, he leaned toward the door and flipped the lock. In the silence of the room, the click sounded erotic.

For a moment, their eyes met and Fiona saw exactly what he was feeling—desire, hot, electric and irresistible. She'd known this was coming from the first moment she'd seen him, but she hadn't known how much she would want it or how little choice she would have to prevent it.

"Now." She wasn't sure who said the word, and she wasn't sure who moved first. All she knew was that his mouth was covering hers. The instantaneous explosion was quick and devastating. There was an aggressiveness to the kiss she hadn't expected—as if he couldn't quite control what was happening, either. Sensations hammered at her as his mouth enticed, seduced, demanded. Her heart pounded in some primitive beat, and an outrageous need streamed through her blood.

When he finally drew back, she gulped in air, feeling singed and shaken. And glorious. Their fingers tangled as they rushed to release clothing.

"Hurry."

"Working on it." As he fumbled with the buttons of her blouse, she tugged the leather jacket down his arms. Slipping her hands beneath his sweater, she ran her hands over the hard ridge of muscle up his back. His strength taunted her, fascinated her.

His hands were no less busy. First her jacket, then her belt hit the floor. A fresh wave of excitement prickled along her skin as her slacks and her panties slid down her legs. Her breath caught when he gripped her waist and lifted her out of them. For a heady instant before he set her down again, she felt powerless, conquered.

Then she was back on her feet and those hands slipped beneath her opened blouse and moved slowly, meticulously from her hips to her breasts. His hands and his gaze lingered there for a moment as if trapped. She couldn't stop herself from trembling.

He met her eyes again. "I want to touch you all over." She nearly cried out when he traced those calloused fingers lightly, thoroughly over her breasts, down her belly and paused at the juncture of her thighs. "I want to taste you, too. Right here."

Her knees buckled, and if he hadn't gripped her hips again, she would have joined her clothes on the floor.

"But I'll have to give you a rain check on that because I want this more." Lifting her slightly, he turned her around. "Brace yourself."

She pressed her hands against the mantle, gripping it tightly when she heard the sound of his jeans unsnapping, his zipper lowering. Need clawed through her.

"Hurry."

"One more thing."

She heard the sound of foil being torn. The backs of his fingers brushed against her as he dealt with the condom. Then he was there, his sheathed penis pressing against her. One of his hands was on her stomach; the other molded itself against her right buttock. Heat seared her at both contact points as he eased her toward him. Using his knees, he widened her stance, and liquid fire pooled in her center when he rubbed the head of his penis against her opening.

"Please." The word came out on a jagged moan.

"Shh." Then his mouth fastened on her shoulder. Heat flashed through her as his teeth nipped.

She bit down hard on her bottom lip, stifling the cry as he pushed into her, farther and farther. And farther. When he reached the hilt, he paused as if determined to hold both of them there. But her climax was already beginning. By the time he withdrew and entered her a second time, her release was rocketing through her.

When she reached the peak, he grasped her more tightly to him, holding her anchored with one hand while he slipped the fingers of the other hand into her folds and found her clitoris. Then he increased the rhythm of his thrusts, back and forth, back and forth. Each time he seemed to fill her more completely. Incredibly, she felt the pressure begin to build again. This climax was longer and harder than the first, and reality seemed to spin away. Dimly, she was aware that he arched back and as he poured himself into her, she shattered.

When she could think again, breathe again, she was still trapped between D.C.'s body and the fireplace and he rested heavily against her. The sound of their ragged breathing filled the small apartment.

Other bits and pieces of reality drifted into her conscious mind. Cool marble pressed against the side of her face, and her knuckles were white where they still gripped the edge of the mantel.

D.C. was still inside of her. Hard and hot. And she still wanted him there. Right there. A flame of desire flared deep inside of her. She'd never felt like this before. So sated. So…sensuously female. And yet, impossibly, she wanted more.

She didn't speak and wondered if she could. Perhaps her vocal chords had been seared by the heat they'd generated. Fiona wasn't sure just how long they stood there, joined, before D.C. sighed and slowly withdrew. She echoed his sigh, and wondered if that was the only sound she was capable of.

"You all right?" D.C. asked.

"Mmm," she managed as he gripped her hips and turned her around. Okay, she was capable of sound. Full words would come next.

His eyes were dark and intense when she met them. And there was a question in them. "That should have taken the edge off. But I'm not through with you. Not nearly."

It gave her some satisfaction that he still seemed as on edge as she felt. "I'm not through with you, either."

"Good." He smiled at her, then brushed his lips against hers. "Gives us both something to look forward to, Lieutenant. Round one was fabulous."

"Agreed."

"You were fabulous." Stepping back, he released her, then scooped up his jacket and moved toward the kitchen where he took care of the condom. By the time he turned back to her, his clothes were in place. Hers weren't.

Not to be outdone by his efficiency, she stepped away from the hearth and gave thanks that her legs held. She made quick work of her clothes and was buttoning her blouse when he picked up the file folder with the clippings.

"If I remember your list correctly, the next stop is the National Gallery," D.C. said. "I've got a plan about how we should handle that."

She shot him a skeptical look. "I'm all ears as long as you remember that I have the final say."

"Yes, Lieutenant." With a grin, he shot her a mock salute before they left the room and climbed the stairs.

7

IT WAS SHORTLY AFTER NOON by the time that Charity Watkins, the tall, blonde woman in charge of the Rubinov exhibit, led Fiona down the long corridor toward the room where the diamond was on display. And Charity was not a happy camper.

Fiona could understand and sympathize with a certain level of annoyance. After all, a nearly priceless necklace had been stolen from the National Gallery on her watch. But from the moment she'd glimpsed Watkins standing just outside the door of her office, she'd also sensed a quick temper and something else.

As much as she hated to admit it, she wished that D.C. hadn't wanted to go off on his own. She would have appreciated his take on the special exhibits director.

The line to get in to see the Rubinov extended down the main hallway of the gallery and all the way out to the street. Though she'd half expected to, Fiona hadn't spotted D.C. standing in it. His "plan" had been to split up once they reached the Smithsonian. That way, he could continue to fly under the radar of both the press and the museum officials, seeing what information he could dig up as typical tourist. He was also going to talk to Bobby Grant, the helpful guard he'd spoken to the day before. Fiona envied him his freedom.

A sign in the open doorway to the exhibition room announced that the current wait to see the Rubinov was one hour. She figured that had been approximately the time it had taken her to get past the press and the TV cameras camped out in front of the gallery and cut her way through a mountain of red tape and two administrative assistants to get into Charity Watkins's inner sanctum.

Once there, she'd been told Ms. Watkins was in a meeting and would be with her shortly. Fiona had checked her watch twice and was debating interrupting the meeting when two women had stepped out into the waiting room. She'd recognized them instantly from the press clipping in Amanda's folder.

The older of the two was Regina Meyers, Gregory Shalnokov's longtime personal assistant. The younger woman was Charity Watkins. The exhibits director wore her straight blond hair loose, and it flowed smoothly down her back in a style that reminded Fiona of Alice in Wonderland. However, the print dress and red blazer had a lot more style than Alice ever had.

The two women were talking in low voices, and Fiona only caught a few of the words.

"Under control…" the older woman said.

"Dollar for…heard that…her fault…outsiders…"

It wasn't so much the words as the tension in the younger woman's voice that made Fiona's eyes narrow in on her. She might have heard more if one of the administrative assistants hadn't entered and said, "Ms. Watkins, Lieutenant Gallagher is here to speak to you."

Both women whirled to face her. Fiona read surprise on Regina's face, but she was almost sure it was fear she saw on Charity Watkins's. Regina hurried forward with her hand extended. "I'm Regina Meyers, and I'm so pleased to have the opportunity to extend Mr. Shalnokov's personal thanks for everything you're doing. Captain Gibbs-Mitchell tells me that we might have lost the Rubinov forever if it hadn't been for you."

Running into Dr. Meyers was a bonus. Fiona took her hand and found herself looking into pale green eyes that held both warmth and sincerity. "I'm happy that the theft wasn't successful."

"Do you have any idea when you'll be making an arrest? I'd like to be able to set Mr. Shalnokov's mind at ease."

"We're investigating several leads." Fiona smiled at the older woman. "I understand that the lock on the display case could only be deactivated by a recording of Mr. Shalnokov's voice. Can you tell me why he insisted on that precaution?"

Something—annoyance perhaps—flickered briefly over Regina's face. "Mr. Shalnokov has his eccentricities. He's always been worried that someone would succeed in taking the Rubinov from him."

"But then why did he put the necklace up for sale at Christie's two years ago?"

Some of the warmth faded from Regina's eyes. "I'm sure he had his reasons. But he quickly changed his mind. He has a very close connection to the stone. I don't believe he ever intends to part with it." With a nod, she said, "I won't take up any more of your time."

"I may need to talk to you again," Fiona said.

Regina took a card from her purse. "Just give me a call."

As Meyers left, Charity Watkins remained in the doorway of her office, blocking the entrance and frowning at Fiona. Her mood didn't improve when Fiona asked to be given a tour of the exhibition.

The room housing the Rubinov was a long rectangular space, and the moment Fiona stepped into it, she knew that D.C. was already there. She felt his presence along her nerve endings.

She hadn't thought, hadn't let herself think about what they'd done in Amanda Hemmings's apartment. But now, the idea of repeating the experience flashed brilliantly into her mind. She felt her heart race and yearning built in her body. And when she found herself scanning the crowd, hoping for a glimpse of him, she ruthlessly turned her attention to Charity Watkins. "Were there this many viewers yesterday?"

"No. There's been a lot more interest since your police department held that press conference this morning."

"You don't sound happy that the exhibit has become even more popular."

Charity stopped and whirled to face her, hostility radiating off of her. "Of course, I'm happy. Everyone should have an opportunity to see the diamond. But because of the publicity, I've spent the morning trying to convince future exhibitors not to cancel."

Was Charity taking some flack for the attempted theft? Was that the reason for the woman's anger?

"Whose idea was it to exhibit the Rubinov here at the National Gallery? Did Mr. Shalnokov approach you, or did you approach him?"

"I approached him," Charity said. "That's part of my job— to research possibilities and to arrange for unusual exhibits. This one took me two years to put together."

"Did you talk to him directly?"

"No. I dealt with his assistant, Regina Meyers. You just spoke with her."

Fiona thought again of what she'd seen and heard. It had smacked of some kind of disagreement. "Did you find it easy to work with her?"

Charity stopped and aimed a frown at her. "Yes. Why do you need to know all of this?"

"Because I'm a cop," Fiona said. "We're insatiably curious. Do you have any idea how someone got the diamond out without setting off any of the alarms? Or without being seen?"

"No. That's *your* job, isn't it?" With that, Charity whirled and continued to walk toward the exhibit, leaving Fiona to wonder how effectively she was handling those waffling future exhibitors. PR did not seem to be Charity Watkins's forte.

Or perhaps she was just seeing her on an off day. Once again, she thought of D.C. and wondered what his take would be.

Their final destination sat on a raised dais at the center of the room. Track lighting illuminated the area, and even at a distance of some ten feet, Fiona caught the glint of blue fire.

More velvet ropes kept viewers several arms' lengths away from the Rubinov. And just in case, there were armed guards stationed at each of the four corners of the dais. That was a change from yesterday.

At a signal from Charity Watkins, one of the guards allowed them access to the roped-off area.

Before they stepped through, Charity spoke in a hushed tone. "You can't touch the glass. If you do the alarm will go off."

"I understand that the lock on the case is voice activated and that only Mr. Shalnokov can open it." Fiona, too, spoke softly, not wanting to draw the attention of the people waiting in line.

"Even then you couldn't get the Rubinov out without setting off the backup alarms."

Unless you had the know-how to jam the whole system at the perfect time. "Then there's a good possibility that it was an inside job."

Every bone in Charity's body stiffened. "I can't imagine that to be true."

It was only as Fiona stepped into the roped-off area that

she caught a glimpse of D.C. in her peripheral vision. He was on the other side of the display case with his back to her. The simple sight of him gave her a sharp sensory shock. His leather jacket was stretched taut over broad shoulders, the cane hung negligently from one arm and his head was slightly inclined toward the guard he was talking to. Even as she absorbed those details, her eyes remained riveted on the Rubinov. It rested on white velvet just below her eye level, and the brilliant blue flame in the stone drew her just as it had before.

She knew the instant that D.C. turned and saw her. Awareness heated her nerve endings, and she raised her eyes to once more meet his over the glass encasing the diamond. For an instant, the fire in the Rubinov seemed to brighten even as her surroundings dimmed. She and D.C. might have been alone in the room. And she was filled with longing. Intense. Inevitable. Was the feeling triggered by the stone? By D.C.? By both?

Fear snaked up her spine. How in the world had she gotten entangled with this? With him? She'd never been the kind of person who had wild, mindless sex up against a fireplace. Now all she had to do was look into his eyes and she wanted to do it again.

She liked straight paths and recognizable destinations. D. C. Campbell was all hairpin curves and sheer drop-offs. But it took all her effort to shift her attention to Charity. The exhibit director's eyes were totally focused on the diamond, and there was something in her expression that was akin to worship.

"It's beautiful, isn't it?" Charity asked in a tone one might use in a church.

"Yes," Fiona replied. Amanda Hemmings didn't seem to be the only one a little obsessed with the Rubinov. "I had a chance to hold it in my hand yesterday. I'll never forget it."

Charity's gaze remained fixed on the necklace. "Neither will I."

"I can't imagine how relieved you must feel that it didn't disappear forever."

"But it will disappear." Charity's rapt expression was replaced with annoyance when the woman turned to face her. "Tomorrow at closing time, it will go back to the private collection of Gregory Shalnokov."

D.C. WATCHED FIONA, unable to redirect his gaze, until the Rubinov was no longer between them. As their eyes had locked over the diamond, his mind had once again been wiped clean. The crowd, the chatter of voices had faded, even the voice of the man at his side—everything had disappeared. For that small stretch of time, he'd lost track of himself, of where he was or why he'd come here. There'd only been Fiona.

He should be getting used to the effect she had on him. She fascinated him, enchanted him in a way no other woman ever had—or ever would. In a way, she was as intriguing a puzzle as the case they were working on. And she was finally beginning to open up to him, revealing pieces of herself. But it wasn't enough.

Oh, he was beginning to get a clear enough picture of the loneliness of her childhood. When he compared it to his own, to the family who had always surrounded him and supported him, his heart twisted for her. He could understand why she'd built up walls. Just as he was beginning to understand why Christmas wasn't her favorite holiday. He had some ideas about changing that. And there was more she could tell him, more he wanted her to share—until every last barrier between them was broken down.

She'd gotten to him. No, more than that, she'd gotten inside of him. He'd known her what…? Less than twenty-four hours, and she'd invaded his system.

What had happened in that small apartment when he'd made love to her still baffled him. As much as he prided himself on being able to improvise, taking a woman up against a fireplace wasn't his usual style. Not that he was sorry he'd done it.

No, what bothered him was the fact that he simply hadn't been able to wait. The sense of urgency she aroused in him every time he touched her was unprecedented. And having her should have sated his desire for her. At least temporarily. But in the hour he'd spent away from her, he hadn't been able to keep her from slipping into his thoughts.

Without any conscious intention on his part, his gaze dropped to the blue diamond. He thought again of the legend. Fiona might not buy into it, but he wasn't sure it could be so easily dismissed. He'd traveled enough, seen enough things to respect the power places and objects could possess—especially when people bought into them. Many of the men who'd served under him had worn a talisman—a medal, a photo of a loved one—and credited it with saving their lives.

For his own part, he was much more likely to believe that the blue stone had the power to elicit obsession, greed and death than love.

"You all right?"

D.C. dragged his attention back to Bobby Grant. Lucky for D.C., the security guard had been stationed at the entrance so he hadn't had to wait in line.

D.C. inclined his head toward Fiona and the blonde. "How come they get to be up close and personal with the diamond?"

Bobby grinned slowly. "I guess you ain't been watchin' the news. There's a TV in our break room that runs 24/7. Ever since this morning, all the media are talking about is

the attempted theft of the Rubinov. The good-looking bru-
nette is the cop assigned to the case, and the blonde is
Charity Watkins. She's director of the gallery's special exhibits."

D.C. kept his eyes on Fiona as Watkins led the way to the
service door at the back of the room. He recognized the other
woman immediately. The long swing of blond hair was hard
to miss. She'd been the one who'd drawn his mother's attention as they'd left the National Gallery yesterday.

"I suppose Ms. Watkins is taking a lot of heat for the theft?"

Bobby shrugged. "Can't say. But there's a lot of pressure
on the people heading up security. They're doubling the
number of guards on all shifts."

"You were on duty at closing time yesterday, right? Did
you see anything out of the ordinary?"

Bobby shook his head. "I been asked that question by the
insurance investigator and by my supervisor. We did what we
always do. We checked to make sure the room was empty,
turned out the lights and then locked up."

"I assume that there's some lag between the time the
exhibits shut down and the gallery clears."

"About half an hour."

"Any details stand out in your mind about yesterday?"

Bobby considered the question for a minute. "We had several
busloads of school kids on field trips. But we were briefed
about them. Kids get antsy, touch things. You have to be alert."

"Anything else?"

"We had some viewers who were dressed in Santa hats and
red scarves. I might have spotted four of them. All of them
were young, two were women. I thought at first they might
be chaperones with one of the school groups. One of the
women wore thick-soled black boots that laced all the way up

to the knees. The other was a small blonde passing out brochures about a toy drive."

Not much got by Bobby, D.C. figured. He inclined his head to where Fiona was now standing with Charity Watkins. "If I were going to rob the place, I'd come in through the service doors right after lockup, then exit through those same doors and find a way to disappear into the group visitors still on their way out."

Bobby gave the doors a thoughtful glance. "Not a bad plan. But only high-level employees can get in through there. They don't even give the code out to the guards. And then infrared security beams are turned on once the doors are locked."

"They could have been switched off," D.C. murmured.

"All that is handled in the main security room. We have to have the room cleared and locked down by five sharp."

D.C. pictured it in his mind. Once the alarms were jammed, you could nip in the service doors, unlock the case and switch the necklaces. He figured sixty to eighty seconds—two minutes if you had to deactivate the lock with a recording of Shalnokov's voice.

Once the alarms were up and the cameras back on, everything would look totally in order. The fake necklace would be right there in the display case.

"You're thinking it had to be an inside job by someone who knew the security inside out," Bobby said.

Yes, Bobby was a sharp one. "Possibly." He slipped a card out of his pocket and handed it to the guard. "Do me a favor and give me a call if you think of anything else."

Bobby shot D.C. a curious glance. "Is the army investigating the attempted theft, too?"

"Not officially. I'm curious. Things are a little slow over at Fort McNair."

Bobby smiled at him. "I imagine anything would be slow after being in Iraq."

With a final nod to the guard, D.C. turned.

"One other thing, Captain."

When he turned back, Bobby motioned him closer. "One of those people wearing Santa hats—the woman handing out brochures—was among the last to leave. I remember seeing her run down the front steps just as we were closing the doors. It must have been close to five-thirty."

"Thanks. I owe you." Then, turning away from the guard, D.C. made his way against the flow of traffic headed toward the display case. He wanted a closer look at the service door. Chance would no doubt have the particulars, but he couldn't help wondering how long it would take to crack the code. Probably too long. It would be much easier if someone had the code already.

The two women were standing in the open doorway now. Fiona's questions were brief and to the point. Charity Watkins stood there, her arms crossed. The fingers of one hand tapped impatiently against her arm. It was the same stance she'd taken with the group of children yesterday. Was it anger? Or nerves?

He watched Fiona raise one of her hands to press it briefly against her temple. A headache, he guessed and frowned. Little wonder—she hadn't eaten more than two bites of that blueberry scone all day.

He was close enough now to see that the hallway beyond the door was narrow and a nearby window looked out on the sculpture garden one story below. How far was it to an exit?

"Does the public have access to this area?" Fiona was asking.

"No. Only staff," Charity Watkins replied. "It's rarely used. On opening nights, exhibitors often throw preview parties, and servers will use these doors."

"Who caters these parties?"

Charity waved an impatient hand. "The staff at our café handles it. But someone from security would be in charge of letting them in."

As they stepped back into the exhibition room, Charity glanced pointedly at her watch. "If that's all—"

"Did you personally visit the exhibition yesterday?"

"Yes." Annoyance flickered over her face. "It's part of my job to see that everything runs smoothly."

"How many times did you come in here?"

Charity's eyes narrowed. "Three or four."

"And the last time?"

"Shortly before the room closed. I'm sure all of my visits were recorded on the security tapes. Now, if we're through here…"

Fiona nodded at her. "Thanks for your help."

As the woman hurried away, D.C. moved close enough to Fiona to murmur, "Nice work, Lieutenant. She didn't like being questioned about her visits to the exhibit."

They exited the room and started toward the front doors of the gallery. "She didn't like being questioned about anything. But she was already in a bad mood when I got here. She'd been talking with Regina Meyers, Shalnokov's personal assistant. And I'm pretty sure the snit she's in stems from that meeting."

"Interesting."

"I could understand her mood better if Shalnokov had threatened to close the exhibit. But he didn't. And the diamond is back in the display case. If I were in charge of this exhibit, I'd be doing a happy dance."

Just short of the exit doors, D.C. put a hand on Fiona's arm. "Could be she's miffed because she's one of the people you and Chance are looking at."

"Well, it makes sense, given that she's thoroughly familiar

with the security surrounding the diamond. She could have opened the security doors."

"I'd like to think she had something to do with it, too, except that my mother and sister and I can provide her with an alibi that's probably backed up by security tape. At the crucial time period—between 4:50 p.m. and 5:10 p.m., she was having a little confrontation with some school children right about where we're standing."

Fiona frowned. "She could have given the code to someone else, and then made sure she had an alibi."

Brows raised, he studied her. "I like the way your mind works. Now all we have to do is prove it."

"Spoilsport."

He grinned. "There are other possibilities. Since we're here, why don't we revisit the crime scene?"

"It's not on our to-do list," Fiona said.

"My friend Bobby, the security guard, told me that there was a small, blond woman wearing a Santa hat and a red scarf who was handing out brochures. He places her among the last to exit the building, running down the steps just as the doors were being closed at about five-thirty."

"And she went right to the sculpture garden." Fiona rubbed at her temple again.

He was going to take care of that.

"The timing is just about perfect. I'd like to take another look at it. Maybe get a new angle?"

"Sure. Okay."

"I'll meet you in there in ten minutes."

8

WHILE D.C.'S TEN MINUTES STRETCHED CLOSE to twenty, Fiona dug her hands into her pockets and studied the area blocked off by the crime scene tape. Fifteen yards to her left, the ice rink was full. Above the muted sounds of chatter and laughter, a tenor crooned his dreams for a white Christmas.

In front of her, the afternoon sun glared off the few inches of snow still stubbornly clinging to the ground. If the temperatures held, a white Christmas might be in the cards for Washington. Narrowing her gaze, Fiona focused her attention on the spot where she'd first seen Amanda Hemmings the night before. The headache that had been a niggling little annoyance when they'd arrived at the gallery had blossomed into a throbbing ache. And she knew the cause—lack of sleep and the frustration at how little progress they were making.

While she'd been waiting for D.C., she'd made three calls on her cell, the first to Natalie. Chance wanted to meet with them at six to share information. Next she'd checked in on Amanda's condition at the hospital. No change. But there'd been a visitor, someone who'd identified himself as Amanda's cousin. The desk nurse's description matched the way General Eddinger had described Billy Franks.

The question was, how had Amanda's cousin learned that

she was in the hospital unless he knew she'd been mugged the night before?

Frustrated, she whirled to face the gate she'd entered through. Where was D.C.? Her third call had been to his cell, but he'd let it roll into voice mail. It both annoyed and baffled her that she wanted to talk with him, to get his take on what little she'd learned. She'd worked with partners before, but she'd never meshed quite so quickly with anyone else. And she was beginning to like him and to value his judgment. There was no denying that she was beginning to have feelings for him. And she knew how quickly feelings could complicate things.

Besides, she should be thinking about the case. Cold stung her cheeks as she turned back to the area roped off by the tape. Once more, she replayed the scenario D.C. had described in her mind. He'd first spotted Amanda along a path that led to an entrance on the corner of Madison Drive and Seventh Avenue. But she'd moved off the path, quickly dodging between trees and shrubs until she reached the four-sided pyramid.

"Got it figured out yet?"

Whirling, Fiona absorbed a sharp jolt of pleasure as D.C. filled the opening of the gate, stepped through it, then used his cane to shut it behind him. In spite of his injury, he moved gracefully and efficiently across the uneven ground.

He had the collar of his coat turned up against the chill. The dark hair and dark clothes made a striking contrast against the snow-covered ground.

"You're late," Fiona said.

He hefted the paper bag he carried in his hand. "I come bearing gifts. But first, tell me what you're thinking."

She turned back to the sculpture. "I'm still wondering why this particular place. If she was running away, I guess this is one of the few pieces of art in here that would provide good cover."

Folding her arms across her chest, she began to tap her fingers on her arm. "But its size also makes it easy to find. Perhaps she was supposed to meet someone and hand off the diamond."

"Good points. Her assailant could have been waiting for her. I didn't see him enter. He was just suddenly there."

"If she was running away, why not get closer to the skaters or to the café? There's safety in numbers."

"But she would have been more easily seen. And in that hat and scarf, she'd be recognizable." D.C. frowned as he scanned the fence and line of trees that ran behind the pyramid. "Maybe the man who attacked her saw her dash in here and used a different entrance. The trees provided cover and gave him an opportunity to sneak up on her."

Fiona frowned. "And if it was a planned rendezvous spot and she was supposed to hand off the diamond, why did he attack her?"

"Because she'd pulled a double cross and was running away? Or because she was trying to stop the robbery?"

Fiona turned her frown on him. "That's certainly the scenario that your general would like."

"Just trying to keep my mind open to all the possibilities."

"I checked with the hospital. There's no change in her condition, but a young man identifying himself as her cousin visited Amanda at the hospital."

D.C. smiled at her. "So now we can add Billy Franks to our to-do list."

"My thoughts exactly."

When she started past him, D.C. stepped into her path. She came up hard against him and his free arm came around her. "Whoa. Not so fast."

She glanced up at him, more aware than she wanted to be of how hard his body was and how much she wanted to stay pressed against it. She eased herself away. "If you want to work with me, you have to keep up."

He rattled the bag he was carrying. "You didn't have lunch on your to-do list, so I figured we could take a break and have a winter picnic." He nudged her to a nearby bench.

"A winter picnic?"

"Yeah. We used to have them all the time when I was a kid. After my dad died, my mom tried to create special family events on the weekends. Sometimes, it would involve going to the movies. In the summer we'd go fishing or spend a day at the beach. And in the winter, we'd pick a special destination like the zoo or we'd end up here at the National Mall. She'd pack sandwiches and thermoses of hot chocolate. One time we came, it was just a few days before Christmas."

Fiona could picture it clearly in her mind. The laughter, the cold. "It sounds like fun."

He met her eyes. "It was. That's why I thought you might enjoy it. We've taken a pretty fast trip, Fiona. We haven't even had a date."

Her eyes narrowed. "I don't mind the speed, and I don't need a date."

"Maybe I do."

Fiona wasn't sure what to say to that. He set the bag down between them and began unpacking. Paper-wrapped hamburgers, packets of French fries. Her eyes widened at the sheer amount of the food.

"Don't you ever stop eating?"

"It's been hours since those doughnuts." He pulled a bottle of water and a packet of aspirin out of the bag. "First things first. This is step one in Dr. Campbell's cure for the common headache."

"I'm fine."

"Liar. You're as frustrated as I am that we're not making more progress, not to mention the fact that the evidence is piling up against Private Hemmings."

Since she couldn't argue with that, she took the packet, ripped it open and downed the pills.

"Now for the protein. That's step number two."

Before she could object, she found herself holding a hamburger. "I usually don't eat—"

"Lunch or much breakfast, either. But I have to keep up my strength, and it would be rude for me to eat alone. Besides, I'll just keep nagging you." He picked up a packet of French fries and offered it to her.

Fiona took one and bit into it.

D.C. unwrapped his own hamburger. "I thought of getting you a spinach salad. But you only ate half a scone for breakfast so I opted for meat and potatoes."

He had the sandwich halfway to his mouth when he turned to her. "Tell me you're not a vegetarian."

Fiona's lips twitched. "I'm not a vegetarian." Then to prove it, she bit into the burger. The combination of juicy meat, sharp cheese and tangy dill had her quickly taking another bite.

"Good?" D.C. asked.

"Mmm," was all Fiona could manage to mumble.

He handed her a napkin. "Why did you become a cop?"

She shook her head. "This is date talk, right?"

"Busted."

He'd brought the food, so she supposed she could go with the flow. She took another bite of her burger and gave it some thought. "I saw it as a way of making a difference. How about you? Why did you become an MP?"

"I like solving puzzles, even when I'm in the middle of a case like this, when we seem to be turning over stone after stone with no result."

She met his eyes, and the understanding she saw in them did more than the aspirin to ease her headache.

"We're going to find something, Fiona. I'm betting that the diamond was taken out of the exhibition room through those service doors. But even with the code, someone would have had to hack into the security system and either shut it off or delay the start-up—at least for the length of time it would take to get into the case and switch the necklaces," D.C. said.

"So that means we're right back where we started. Whoever is behind this had to be a real pro or an extremely talented amateur," Fiona pointed out.

"I'm leaning toward a combination of both. What we've got here sort of boils down to two sets of suspects. We know there had to be someone on the inside. The timing of the switch in that exhibition room had to be very precise. Then we have the probable involvement of Amanda Hemmings and three others who were rank amateurs. We could go with the theory that Billy had the expertise to jam the security system. And let's say Amanda's job was to get the diamond out of the National Gallery. We still have to account for the recording of Shalnokov's voice—and for someone on the inside who knew the security procedures."

Fiona bit into a French fry. "Say you have the perfect plan to rob the National Gallery, why involve amateurs like Billy and Amanda?"

"Maybe they had to."

"No matter which way we try to spin it, Amanda Hemmings is in the thick of it."

"I agree. The question is how is she involved?"

Fiona traded her half-eaten hamburger to D.C. for more French fries.

"Arthur Franks could be the one pulling all their strings. But he's not going to admit it." D.C. licked ketchup off his thumb, then began to gather their wrappers and stuff them into the empty paper bag. "Even if Chance gets us permission to visit him, it's highly unlikely he'll tell us anything. So let's go question Billy."

She started to rise, but D.C. moved quickly. He cupped the back of her neck with one hand and tilted up her chin with the other.

"What's a winter picnic without dessert?" He lowered his head just enough to nip her bottom lip.

Fiona heard her breath shudder out. With it went any will to resist.

He took her mouth slowly as if he were indeed sampling some rich, forbidden dessert. With just the tip of his tongue he traced her lips, lingering at each corner, mingling his breath with hers.

She was losing ground, sinking deeper and deeper into an airless world. The music from the ice rink changed rhythm and tempo until it was beating as fast as her heart. A cold breeze rattled the paper bag that still lay between them on the bench, but all she was aware of was the heat that radiated through her from his hands.

He captured her bottom lip with his teeth and nibbled, then drew it into his mouth to suck until she began to tremble, and an ache began to build inside of her. She placed a hand on his chest, felt the cool leather beneath her palm and the rapid pulse of his heart beneath.

In some part of her mind, she knew she should push him away. But she wouldn't. She couldn't. Instead, with a moan that was half surrender, half demand, she pressed her mouth fully to his. Arousal exploded into passion in the instant of full contact. And she slid deeper into a world where there was only him.

It cost him to pull back, to force himself to remember where they were. Her eyes were clouded, her cheeks flushed, her mouth still swollen from his sensual assault. He released her before he gave into the temptation to kiss her again.

When her eyes finally focused, he read a mix of desire and confusion—a pretty close match to what he was feeling. He captured one of her hands and raised it to his lips. "I'm sorry it's winter. And I'm even sorrier we're not alone."

"I don't understand this."

"Ditto." But he suspected he was beginning to. He thought of those two moments in the exhibition room when they'd stood, their gazes locked, with only the Rubinov separating them. He thought of the legend, and once again, he couldn't discount it. Something crawled up his spine. He recognized it as the same feeling that had always served him well as a kid, that feeling of imminent danger that he'd experienced when he'd first sensed her presence in the sculpture garden.

He'd known her less than twenty-four hours, but no other woman had ever been so important to him. So necessary.

For now, he pushed the thought aside. They had work to do.

Gathering up their trash and his cane, he rose, then held out his free hand to Fiona. "C'mon, Lieutenant. Let's go turn over another stone.

BILLY FRANKS LIVED on the second floor of an older three-story building within walking distance of the main campus of American University. A small sign out front advertised efficiency apartments. Luck had been with them, and a tenant had been leaving just as they'd been about to ring Billy's apartment.

As they climbed the stairs, Fiona said, "Remember, I'm taking the lead on this one."

"Sure," D.C. said. They'd discussed their strategy on the way over. She was going to introduce him as Captain Campbell and they were going to try to sidestep the issue of his being stationed at Fort McNair and knowing Amanda. He was perfectly willing to take a backseat because that would leave him free to observe and figure out exactly what role he would play.

She stopped at the top of the stairs and turned to face him. "Since I'll be doing most of the talking, is there anything in particular that you'd like me to ask?"

D.C. bit back a grin. "You don't trust me to stay in the background."

"I think that if you sense an opportunity, you'll run with it. I'd like to avoid that, if possible. So if you have a question…?"

"Other than how he found out his cousin was in the hospital?"

"Yes."

"I won't know until he answers that one."

She sighed. "D.C., I would prefer not to spook him."

"I'll try to keep my inner bad cop under control."

"Do that." Turning abruptly, she led the way down the short hallway to apartment 207, then knocked on the door.

Footsteps approached and the door opened the length of the security chain. "Yes?"

Over Fiona's shoulder, D.C. saw a young man with longish dark hair, wearing a black turtleneck, jeans and glasses. He fit the descriptions they'd received from General Eddinger, the desk nurse, and Amanda's landlady to a T.

Fiona held out her badge. "Are you Billy Franks?"

"Yes."

"I'm Lieutenant Gallagher and this is Captain Campbell. We're here to ask you about your cousin, Amanda Hemmings. Can we come in?"

"Sure." He shut the door, released the chain and then opened it again. The apartment was small and narrow with a kitchen at one end and an open door leading to a bathroom at the other. But it was what filled the room that caught D.C.'s interest.

Billy Franks had company. And the dress code for the day was head-to-toe black. Not that D.C. could argue with it.

A young man with carrot-red hair sat at one of two computers on a long table that stretched the length of one wall. He was busily clicking himself out of screens. The girl sitting on the couch closed a laptop. She wore her dark hair pulled into two ponytails. But it was her feet that drew D.C.'s attention. She wore thick soled black boots laced to the knees.

Pulling out his notebook, D.C. moved to the one computer that was still open to a screen. Once he'd noted the URL, he turned, rested his hip against the table and waited.

Fiona turned to him. "If you wouldn't mind taking notes, Captain?"

"Not at all."

Fiona sent a smile at all three of the young people. "Sorry to interrupt. This shouldn't take long. Are you classmates?"

"Yes." Billy sat on the arm of the sofa. "We're studying together."

Out of the corner of his eye, D.C. watched a puzzled expression bloom on Fiona's face.

"Aren't you all on winter break?"

Carrottop flicked a glance at the girl, but Billy replied without missing a beat. "We're doing an independent study project for one of our professors."

"Wow! That's dedication. And your professor's name is?"

"Lewen. Kathryn Lewen. What does this have to do with my cousin?"

"Do you mind if I sit down?" Without waiting for a reply, she grabbed the chair near D.C. and turned it around so that she could keep all three of them in view. Then she said to Billy, "Why don't you introduce me to your study mates."

Billy inclined his head towards Carrottop first. "Mark Dillinger." And then pointing to the girl, he added, "Carla Mason."

"Nice to meet you," Fiona said. Then she turned her attention to Billy. "What can you tell me about Amanda Hemmings?"

"Not much. She got in touch with me a couple of months ago. We've gone out together a few times."

He was smart, D.C. thought. But not a good enough actor to make his speech sound unrehearsed.

"We were supposed to meet today for an early lunch. When I went over to her place, her landlady told me that she'd been mugged. I called all the hospitals in the area until I found her. The nurse only let me see her for a moment. Amanda didn't recognize me."

Neat story, D.C. thought. He didn't doubt for a minute that Billy Franks knew how to dot his *I*s and cross his *T*s.

Fiona let out a sigh. "Well, that explains it. I was wondering how you learned that she'd been hurt. There hasn't been any mention of it on the news."

"You've been on the news. You're investigating that attempted robbery at the Smithsonian, aren't you?" Billy asked.

"I'm looking into it."

His eyes narrowed as if a sudden thought had struck him. "Is my cousin Amanda involved in that?"

The question was better than the little speech, D.C. noted.

Fiona widened her eyes. "Do you have any reason to believe she might be?"

He shook his head. "Not really. But she couldn't stop talking about that diamond." He glanced at his friends. "She was close to obsessed with it."

Carla and Mark nodded in unison.

"She was doing some volunteer work at the Mall," Billy continued, "and she said she'd been in to see it several times. When I visited her apartment, she had this file of all the stories printed in the newspapers. She was going to make a scrapbook."

"How about you?" Fiona asked. "Have you been to see it?"

"No. Diamonds aren't my thing."

Fiona turned to Carla and Mark. "How about you two?"

"No," they replied in unison.

"Where were all of you yesterday?"

Carrottop and the girl turned to Billy.

D.C. bit back a smile. They hadn't seen that one coming.

"We were here studying together until around three. Then we took a break and went out," Billy said.

"Where to?" Fiona asked.

"Professor Lewen had a gathering of students at her place, sort of a Christmas open house for those of us who didn't go home for the break."

"Could you give me her address and phone number so that I can verify that?"

"Sure." Billy rattled them off and D.C. made notes.

"Thank you." She glanced at D.C. "Do you have any questions for Billy?"

"No." D.C. flipped his notebook shut. "I'm good."

They were at the door when Billy said, "My cousin. Is she going to be all right?"

Fiona turned back. "The doctors say that she's stable."

"What about her memory?" Billy asked.

"I don't have any information on that."

Fiona waited until they were in the stairwell before she said, "You were a very good boy in there. Thanks."

"You were the one who was good. He didn't see your question about their activities yesterday coming. FYI, he was researching amnesia on the Internet."

"Which he would have explained away as concern about his cousin. If we go with the theory that Amanda isn't faking the amnesia, then it had to have come as quite a shock to Billy."

"And if she is faking it, the visit gave Amanda a chance to fill Billy in."

Fiona pushed through the door to the street. "My gut tells me the three musketeers are involved in the robbery."

He opened the passenger door, then circled the car and climbed in beside her. "My gut's in agreement with yours, but I've got a little more than that. Bobby, the security guard I was talking to at the gallery, described one of the young people wearing Santa hats as also wearing thick-soled boots that laced up to the knees."

"Carla."

"That's what I'm thinking."

Fiona pursed her lips. "It's not proof. We won't even be able to get a search warrant on that alone."

"Then we'll get more. Let's give Professor Lewen a call."

Fiona pulled out her cell and D.C. read the number he'd jotted in his notebook.

After a moment, she met his eyes. "It's busy."

"Want to bet they're nailing down their alibi?"

"We'll have to go visit the professor."

"I have an idea about that."

"What?"

"Trust me."

9

D.C. TOOK A SHARP LEFT at the first corner, then executed a U-turn, inched the car back up to the intersection and stopped. Through the windshield, Fiona could just see the front of Billy Frank's apartment building. She caught a flicker of movement from a window on the second floor. Billy's apartment?

"What are we doing?" she asked.

"A little surveillance."

"I thought we were going to visit Professor Lewen. The address isn't very far from here."

"Let's wait and see."

Less than two minutes later, Billy, Carla and Mark shot out the door and piled into a compact car that had seen better days a decade ago.

Fiona stared at him. "How did you know they'd come out?"

"I had a hunch. And I want to see where they go."

"Too bad it's not the van."

"Nothing worthwhile is that easy." D.C. waited another ten seconds before he eased up to the corner and pulled around it. Two blocks ahead of them, the compact car took a right turn.

Fiona fished out her cell and tapped in numbers. "I have a GPS system on this. Just for fun, let's see how far it is to Professor Lewen's house...ah, six point two miles. Just over the state line in Maryland. And if I were paying her a visit, I would turn just where they did."

They drove in silence until D.C. made another right. The small car was three blocks ahead and turning onto a ramp.

"My laptop is on the backseat," D.C. said. "Why don't you see what you can dig up on Professor Kathryn Lewen?"

Fiona reached for it and started work. She was aware when the car picked up speed on the ramp, but she kept her gaze focused on the screen. "Nice equipment," she murmured as she tapped the keys. "The police department doesn't provide anything quite this fancy."

"Neither does the army. My brother gave that to me. I worked for him briefly about six months ago. I was on leave after I got back from Iraq, and I had some time on my hands."

Fiona wondered if the leave had anything to do with his injury. Whatever had caused the damage to his leg, she knew firsthand from her visits to Walter Reed what the long and grueling process of rehabilitation was like. She didn't want to think about him in a place like that. If she was going to get out of this episode with D.C., she had to at least try to keep things simple.

Pushing the images firmly out of her mind, she concentrated on the computer screen. She quickly located a photo and short biography on American University's Web page. "She's young—I'd guess early to midthirties. Long, curly, light brown hair. She's been a full professor in the Information Studies Department for three years." She glanced at D.C. "They don't offer much more than that. But if the photo is up-to-date, she made full professor in record time."

"Any publications?"

Fiona tapped some keys and felt a little thrill of excitement.

"I found her Web site. Last year she published a full-length book—*Security in a Digital Age.* You can buy it on Amazon."

"I'll ask my brother to dig deeper."

Fiona glanced at him. "You suspect her of playing some role in the robbery."

"She's Billy's professor and he's tight with her. Look, they're stopping."

Fiona glanced through the windshield just in time to see the compact car turn in to a driveway. They were on a tree-lined residential street, where the houses were set on generous lots, well back from the road. Thanks to the afternoon sun, the snow was melting and patches of grass were already visible on the wide lawns. "Her book must be doing well."

D.C. stopped the car. "Do I call the shots on this one or do you?"

Knowing that she might be getting herself into trouble, Fiona said, "I called the last one. And you were the one who thought to follow them. It's your turn."

"You play fair, Lieutenant. I like that." He moved quickly, taking her chin and brushing his lips over hers. The contact was brief, but the effect, a melting sensation that streaked right to her toes, lingered even as she joined him on the sidewalk.

"I wish you'd stop doing that."

"What?"

"Kissing me."

"You don't really mean that." He picked up the ends of her hair and rubbed them between his fingers.

"Yes, I do."

This time it was the heat in his eyes that streaked right through her.

"I'm wondering just how long it would take me to prove you're lying."

Not long. The color rose in her cheeks. "I want you to stop kissing me while we're working."

"Ah. That's a different story."

"Then you'll agree?"

"Nope." Taking her arm, he pulled her into a driveway bordered by a high hedge.

"It's the next house."

"I know that. I just want to try something."

Fiona bit her tongue so that she wouldn't ask what. She'd told him he could take the lead on this one. But she had to bite down even harder when he led the way through a break in the hedge. They emerged on a lawn dotted with trees. The house sat half a football field away and it boasted both front and back porches. A Christmas tree twinkled merrily on the other side of a sliding glass door. Billy and his pals were just filing into the house.

"C'mon." Moving quickly and gracefully in spite of the cane, D.C. drew her with him from tree to tree until they arrived at one side of the glass door.

Through the branches of the Christmas tree, she could see a tall woman lead Billy, Carla and Mark into a spacious room lined with bookshelves. The woman—Kathryn Lewen—had that very curly hair that was hard to tame. In her photo she'd worn it pulled away from her face, but today it fell unchecked halfway down her back. She walked with a long, easy stride, settled herself on a large leather love seat and gestured the other three onto the sofa that faced hers. A fire beckoned warmly on the hearth. Carla and Mark sat. Billy remained standing.

Unlike her three students, Kathryn Lewen was not dressed in black. Instead, she wore earth tones—a long, chocolate-colored skirt, a loosely fitting tan sweater and comfortable looking clogs. Something prickled at the edge of Fiona's mind. There was something familiar about the professor, but Fiona couldn't put her finger on exactly what.

A sudden breeze stung Fiona's cheeks and caused the wind chimes near the back of the house to sound.

"What are we doing?" she whispered.

"Gathering information."

Billy was talking now, but the sound didn't carry through the glass.

"How? We can't hear them," Fiona pointed out.

"The tree is blocking me some, but I can guess at a few words. Police and Rubinov. Suspects."

"You read lips."

"A little."

"You've done this Peeping Tom thing before."

"In my misspent youth. My mom could tell you a few stories. But their body language is interesting, too. What do you see?"

Fiona studied the four people in the room. Mark and Carla sat mute on the couch, just as they had when she and D.C. had visited the apartment. Once again, Billy was doing the talking. Tension radiated from his body and from his staccato gestures.

Kathryn Lewen sat relaxed on the sofa, not moving at all. Fiona took a moment to study her again. "She looks as young as she did on the Web site. And in person, she reminds me of someone. I can't think who."

"Anything else?"

"She's at ease. Perfectly composed. Billy isn't."

"Nerves. He's spooked. The person who attacked Amanda was easily spooked, too. What about the other two?"

"Followers," Fiona said. "Billy's the spokesperson even here."

"That fits, too. I'm betting he's the one who followed Amanda into the sculpture garden while the other two manned the getaway car."

"All of which makes a very nice theory. Let's go see if the professor backs up their alibi. If she doesn't, that will give us something."

"Not enough." Taking her arm, he started around the back of the house. To Fiona's surprise he headed toward another hedge.

"Wait a minute. We have to check their alibi."

"We will. You can call her from the car."

"But we're right..." She broke off as D.C. pulled her through another hedge. "Here."

"We've already spooked them once. If we arrive on their professor's doorstep minutes after they do, they'll get the idea that we think they're involved."

Fiona stopped and waited for him to face her. "And we don't want them to know that because...?"

"We don't have enough hard evidence to link them to the robbery yet. You were the one who didn't want to spook them when we questioned them earlier."

He was right. She studied him for a moment. "You think she's going to back them up, don't you?"

"I do. But she could have several reasons for doing that. They're her students. And she let them into her house. My guess is that she'll want to protect them from being harassed by the police."

"Even if they weren't at her house yesterday?"

"Especially if they weren't at her house."

"You think she's involved?"

"She's the one person who might know if Billy is talented enough to break through the security at the National Gallery. And we don't want to spook her, either. Not yet. At least not until you remember who she reminds you of. Or until Jase finds something."

As they continued down the drive, D.C. called his brother and asked him to run deep background checks on Kathryn Lewen, Charity Watkins and Regina Meyers.

When he was finished, Fiona said, "I can't argue with your logic, but I wouldn't have done it your way."

"I know. But we learned more my way than if we'd just walked up to the door and asked if Billy, Carla and Mark were at her house from three o'clock on yesterday."

Fiona ran a hand through her hair. "I guess we did. Don't you ever take a straight path?"

He slung a friendly arm around her shoulder. "I prefer crooked ones. You never know what's around the next curve."

"YOUR HUNCH WAS RIGHT," Fiona said as she disconnected her cell. "Professor Kathryn Lewen claims that the three musketeers were at her house yesterday from about three-thirty until nine."

D.C. flicked her a glance as he drove the car down a ramp. "You think she was lying?"

"Yes. She seemed totally surprised by the call. That's hard to believe since they're right there in her house, telling her about our visit."

D.C. grinned. "See? We wouldn't have known that if we hadn't done our Peeping-Tom thing through her window."

Fiona might have smiled if she hadn't suddenly realized where they were headed. "This is the way to Billy's apartment."

"Right." He made a left and eased into a parking space directly across from the building.

"Wait." But he was already out of the car. Fiona unhooked her seat belt and scrambled after him. "This is the real reason we didn't ask Kathryn Lewen face-to-face. You planned on coming back here while they were gone."

"This is our chance to get a closer look at those computers."

"No." She clamped a hand on his arm as he stepped off the curb. "I saw that equipment. It's state-of-the-art. If they were skilled enough to hack into the security system at the National Gallery, how much do you want to bet that if you start working on them you'll leave a trail? We need a search warrant."

Frustration shone in his eyes. "You already said we don't have enough to get one. I'm good, Fiona. Give me half an hour and—"

"What happened to the don't-spook-them plan? If they even suspect we're onto them, they'll delete everything. They could even get rid of the equipment, and we'll have nothing." Past his shoulder, she caught a flicker of movement from a window on the second floor. "Besides, Billy has a neighbor who's watching us right now." She tightened her grip on his arm. "Don't look."

"Wouldn't think of it." D.C. steered her across the street. "That was a good catch, Lieutenant."

"I'm not going to let you break into Billy's apartment."

"Relax. I can't fault your logic. We're going to call on the person who's watching us."

"Fine."

"Since I've been so reasonable, I'll take the lead."

If she hadn't been so relieved that he wasn't going to break into Billy's apartment, she might have objected.

D.C. KNOCKED ON THE DOOR of apartment 205 and felt some-one examine him through the peephole. Then the chain rattled and the door opened on a plump woman in jeans and a paint-stained Orioles sweatshirt. She'd twisted her hair onto the top of her head and tucked a paintbrush into the bun. Sprays of crystals dangled from each ear, and a pair of glasses with rhinestone-studded frames perched low on her nose.

For a moment she merely studied the both of them. "If

you're selling something, you're out of luck. My trust fund ran out years ago."

"We're not selling anything," D.C. said with a smile.

"Thought not."

Beyond her, he noted the apartment had the same layout as Billy's, but this one was crammed with an eclectic blend of furniture. Rugs, tables and chairs formed tightly grouped conversation areas. Curio cabinets stuffed with china and glass lined one long wall. A canvas rested on an easel angled toward the window.

The woman shifted her gaze to Fiona. "I've seen you on TV. You're investigating that robbery at the National Gallery."

"We're looking into it," D.C. said. "I'm Captain Campbell and this is Lieutenant Gallagher."

"Wendy Davis." She held out her hand to him and as D.C. grasped it, she continued, "You weren't on TV."

"I'm trying to keep a low profile."

"Too bad." She winked at Fiona as she stepped aside and ushered them in. "I could have used the eye candy."

Wendy cut a path through the furniture and waved them into a sturdy-looking love seat near the window. When she dropped into a rocking chair, a fat tabby cat sprang onto her lap.

D.C. pulled out his notebook. "We visited your neighbor earlier."

Wendy nodded. "Then he and his pals took off and you came back. Is Billy a person of interest in your investigation?"

D.C. glanced up at her. She was smart, and she didn't miss much. "We're pursuing a lot of leads. His cousin was mugged last evening near the National Gallery."

Fiona stiffened slightly, but she didn't say a word.

Wendy's eyes narrowed on D.C. "You think there might be a connection between that and the robbery?"

"We can't discuss the details of our investigation. What can you tell us about Billy Franks?"

She shrugged. "I rarely run into him. He's quiet, keeps to himself, doesn't throw wild parties. If I run out of sugar, he's not the neighbor I would think to borrow from."

D.C. smiled. "I see that you paint over near the window. Can you tell us if Billy's pals are here often?"

Wendy ran her hand over the cat. "In the last month, they've been here nearly 24/7. There's lots of food deliveries—Chinese, Italian. Sometimes the delivery guys buzz the wrong apartment."

"Any other visitors?"

She thought for a minute. "There was a woman who came here a couple of times. Once I was on my way out and saw her at their door. She came again just last week, but she didn't stay long."

"Can you give us a description?" D.C. asked.

"Early to midthirties, tallish. Drab clothes, sensible shoes, long, curly hair. She looked like a professor, but I thought it odd that she'd pay house calls. Professors didn't do that when I was in college."

"Perhaps you could sketch us a picture of the professor?" Fiona asked as she offered her notebook and pen.

Wendy glanced at D.C.

"We'd appreciate it."

She began to sketch. "I only saw her from above or in profile when she was standing in front of Billy Franks's door."

"Can you tell us if Billy and his pals were here yesterday during the day?"

Not looking up from her work, she said, "I didn't hear anything. But I usually don't. I saw them leave about three."

She inclined her head toward the window. "That's what I'd usually notice. And, of course, it gets dark so early now, I don't know when he returned." She studied the notepad, added a few more strokes, then handed it to Fiona. "That's the best I can do."

"Thank you, Mrs. Davis." D.C. rose.

"It's Miss. I took my maiden name back after my divorce."

"If there's anything else you remember, please call my lieutenant."

Fiona handed her a card.

They were at the door when Wendy Davis said, "There was something. It's kind of silly. And probably totally irrelevant."

They both turned back.

"One day last week, I was on my way out and I saw the two geeks at Billy's door. They were wearing red scarves. You've seen how they dress—Goth style—and they were carrying shopping bags. I thought I spotted a Santa hat on the top of one of them. It's probably nothing."

"Thank you, Miss Davis."

Fiona waited until they were out on the street to say, "No, you can't break into Billy's apartment to look for scarves or possible hats, either."

"Wouldn't think of it. I imagine they dumped them shortly after they realized Amanda didn't make it home last night. Her landlady certainly didn't mention them." As they crossed the street, he draped an arm across her shoulder and gave it a squeeze. "By the way, you were a very good girl in there."

She shot him a glance. "The eye candy was working. Miss Davis wouldn't have tried to remember half as much for me."

"Yeah, but I wasn't the one who asked her to make a sketch of the mystery woman. Anyone we know?"

"She drew a pretty good likeness of Kathryn Lewen."

He studied the sketch Fiona held out to him. Wendy Davis had drawn the woman in profile. The hair was similar except in the drawing it was pulled back and fastened.

"So we have a neighbor who can probably testify that a professor from American University visited the apartment of one of her students a couple of times," Fiona said. "She also makes them welcome in her home. Big whoop!"

He shot her a glance. "We've just gathered more pieces of the puzzle. We make a good team."

"I can't imagine why you'd think so." Fiona tucked her notebook back into her purse. "Do you really think Kathryn Lewen worked with Billy and the others to steal the Rubinov necklace?"

"I think it's a theory that needs exploring." At the car he turned to face her. "As different as our styles might be, we're both cops."

Fiona sighed. "I wish Wendy Davis had given us more."

"Me, too. What's next on your to-do list? I was thinking we could swing by the hospital to check on Amanda and then go back to your office so you can update Natalie. And we have that meeting with Chance at six. Or…"

Her eyes narrowed. "Or what?"

He gave her hair a gentle tug. "You could go back up and lure Wendy Davis away from the window while I take a look through Billy's apartment."

"No way." But she smiled. "You're trying to cheer me up."

It might have been the expression on her face. It might have been because they were beginning to make some headway on the case. Or it might simply have been that he couldn't help himself. Propping his cane against the car door, he clasped her shoulders, pulled her up on her toes and closed his mouth over hers.

One more taste. Just something to tide him over until he could get her alone and in bed.

Then her lips parted and she wrapped her arms around him. The sound of her moan vibrated through his system. The fact that she seemed as powerless as he was had him pulling her closer until they made one long shadow on the sidewalk.

This time it was the sweetness of her flavor that trapped him. He didn't think of sugar, but of thick, wild honey, the kind that had always melted slowly in his mouth. There was a depth and richness here that grew each time he returned.

More.

He wasn't sure if he said the word against her mouth or merely thought it. Changing the angle of the kiss, he dove in and took them both deeper until he could have sworn that lights exploded in his head. Fire definitely swept through his blood. He couldn't find a word to capture what she did to him. Arousal was too tame, excitement too bland. All he knew was that each time he kissed her, an urgency took hold of him that threatened to take total command. There was nothing but her—her arms, her lips, that slim, strong body. She was all he wanted.

He wasn't aware that he'd hauled her off her feet and settled her on the hood of his car until the sound of a horn penetrated and brought him back to the time and the place.

Head still spinning, he lowered her gently to the sidewalk, then dropped his hands and took two steps back. He didn't grab women, haul them off their feet, and nearly make love to them on the hood of his car.

Not in broad daylight.

"I…" He wanted to apologize. "I…" Shock rocketed through him. It was the second time she'd left him at a loss for words.

Fiona straightened her coat and pushed her hair back. The

fact that she was leaning against the fender of his car for support steadied him a little.

Reaching for his cane, she handed it to him and met his eyes. He read heat, desire and a challenge. "Was that more dessert?"

Admiration shot through him, along with another emotion he'd consider later. For now, he managed a smile. "I was thinking of it more in terms of an appetizer. This day has to end sometime."

10

AN HOUR LATER, D.C. sat across a desk from Fiona while she talked to someone from Walter Reed. Their trip to the hospital had produced nothing. Amanda's condition hadn't changed, and the psychiatrist consulting on her amnesia was prohibiting visitors for twenty-four hours.

D.C.'s brother Jase was running deeper checks on Charity Watkins, Professor Kathryn Lewen and Dr. Regina Meyers, and he was hoping to hear back soon. Amanda Hemmings and Billy Franks had to be involved in this, but D.C.'s instincts told him that the young people's actions were just the tip of the iceberg.

D.C. let his gaze sweep Fiona's small office that was cramped even further by the boxes of toys that were stacked nearly to the ceiling along three walls. In spite of that, the place was ruthlessly organized. The drawers of two file cabinets were closed and neatly labeled. An inbox on her desk held three files, the outbox was empty, and a desk calendar, opened to the correct page, held neatly scripted notations in what looked to be some kind of personal shorthand.

He might have found the room claustrophobic, but the fourth wall was glass and offered a view of the bull pen. Fiona's closed door barely muffled the chatter of voices, an occasional shout or the incessant ringing of phones. As he watched, a detective escorted a handcuffed man to a chair, then sat down behind his desk and booted up his computer. The busy, bordering on chaotic, atmosphere appealed to D.C. far more than the quiet of his own office at Fort McNair.

His cell phone rang just as Fiona hung up hers. When he heard his brother's voice, D.C. pressed the button for speaker phone. "My partner's listening. What do you have?"

"As per your request, I've run background checks on Charity Watkins, Kathryn Lewen and Regina Meyers. So far, they're all clean. But I discovered something on Watkins and Lewen you might find interesting."

"Spill it," D.C. said.

"They're sisters, fraternal twins. Watkins's maiden name is Lewen. Five years ago, while she was still in graduate school, she married an older man, Martin Watkins. He was rich, socially connected and served on the board of directors at the National Gallery at the time Charity went to work there. When he died a year later, she kept his name. She and her sister Kathryn were raised in Kansas by an aunt, one Martha Lewen. Their mother's name was Kate Lewen. No mention of a father on the birth certificate. You can give me a round of applause now."

Laughing, D.C. complied and Fiona joined him.

"Everything checks out so far on Regina Meyers. I'll keep checking, but so far her life is a well-documented open book."

"Can you check Kathryn Lewen's book on digital security and give me a read on just how good she is?" D.C. asked.

"You want to know if she could have breached the security at the National Gallery?" Jase asked.

"Yeah. And it would be really nice if she owned a van."

"Will do."

As he disconnected the call, Fiona began to tap her pencil on her notebook. "So now we've got a link between someone who had inside knowledge of the security surrounding the diamond and access to the code on the service door and someone we can link to Billy Franks. But they all have alibis for the time of the robbery."

"So far," D.C. said. "Amanda may be able to help us break one of them."

"Except she has amnesia," Fiona said as she rose and walked around her desk to join him.

"What if she isn't faking it?" D.C. took her hands in his.

"I didn't say she was."

"Okay. Let's agree for the moment that the amnesia's real." She studied him for a minute. "What are you thinking?"

"If we're going to see her tomorrow morning, it might prove interesting if we took something along to jog her memory."

Fiona narrowed her eyes, the way she often did when she was thinking. He waited, saying nothing, and he could tell the minute she thought of it.

"The necklace. Not the real one. But Chance must still have the copy."

"Good idea."

"It was *your* idea. You just waited for me to catch up."

He leaned down to kiss just the tip of her nose. "I knew you would. Let's go see if Chance can help us out."

HE'D KISSED HER. Just on the tip of her nose, but her office was like a fishbowl, and Fiona was very aware of the interested glances from colleagues as she led the way across the bull pen to the conference room where Natalie and Chance were waiting for them. She knew D.C. well enough now that she ought to be able to anticipate his moves. And he had some fast ones. But she didn't seem to be able to think quickly enough to block him.

Because she didn't want to?

As she stepped into the room, Fiona saw Natalie sitting at one end of a conference table, and Chance leaning against the only wall not currently stacked with toys. There were two unopened files on the table.

Fiona studied Natalie. She looked paler and very uncomfortable. "Are you all right?"

"I'll be better after I unload this baby. But nothing's imminent. Unfortunately."

Chance moved behind Natalie and placed his hands on her shoulders. "The truth is she'd like to be working on this case."

"If I could move." She glanced up at her husband as one of her hands closed over his.

Fiona felt a little pang at the intimacy of the gesture. She'd always dreamed of that kind of closeness. But hadn't she given up that fantasy? She was perfectly happy with her life the way it was.

"I apologize for the fact that we're meeting in here. But it's Fiona's fault." She gestured toward the walls of toys. "My office is also being used for toy storage. This is the only room we could all fit in."

"How are you going to wrap them all?" D.C. asked.

"My volunteers are coming in tomorrow," Fiona replied.

"On the twenty-third? That's cutting it pretty close," D.C. said. "Present wrapping is something my mother used to start at least a month before the big day."

"I suspect my mother started even earlier," Chance said. "But she did it all in secret. Otherwise I would have opened everything long before Christmas morning."

"My mom was a last-minute kind of person," Natalie commented. "I think she used to stay up all night Christmas Eve wrapping presents. Of course, my sisters and I never knew a thing about it. Thanks to my mom, Sierra and Rory and I believed in Santa for a very long time."

Christmas talk. This was one of the reasons she avoided Christmas parties. She always got the same feeling she had when she was growing up—that she was an outsider looking in.

D.C.'s hand slipped around hers. "I think you might need some Christmas elves to help you wrap all of these."

Fiona gave the toys an anxious glance. "We have a lot of volunteers." Hopefully, everyone would show up. "Then we have to transport them." She turned to D.C., and her heart skipped a beat at the understanding she saw in his eyes. "Could the army help with that?"

"Sure. I'll make some calls," he said.

Natalie looked from one to the other. "You seem to make a good team."

"We're getting there." Clearing her throat, Fiona delivered a report on their progress so far.

"Good work," Natalie commented. "Establishing a link between the two sisters and ultimately to Billy Franks is real progress."

"Our circle of suspects may be widening, but the evidence is still pretty overwhelming against Amanda Hemmings."

"You'll see her again in the morning?" Natalie asked.

"Yes. And D.C. and I have an idea. We'd like to take the copy of the Rubinov with us and see if it jogs her memory."

Chance smiled slowly. "I like it. I'll get it to you first thing in the morning."

Natalie glanced at Chance. "Why don't you fill them in on what you've got so far?"

"One of the avenues I'm pursuing is finding out who made the copy. I showed it to the gemologist who authenticated the stone, and he was impressed with the workmanship. Fortunately, I've made some contacts over the years who might be able to point us in the right direction. They're putting out some feelers."

"Considering the Rubinov necklace has been in Shalnokov's private gallery up until this week, wouldn't even the best craftsman have to see it in person to copy it?" D.C. asked.

Chance exchanged a look with his wife. "I told you he was good."

And he was, Fiona thought. That aspect of the case hadn't yet occurred to her. "But you said it was up for auction at Christie's two years ago. Someone could have studied it then. There must have been pictures in the catalogue."

Chance opened one of the files, took out some photos and placed them on the table.

D.C. and Fiona examined the pictures together. To Fiona's mind, they seemed detailed. But she thought of the night before, when she'd held the necklace in her hand and carried it close to her body. "These likenesses are good, but it wouldn't be the same as holding it, feeling the weight of it, examining the original designer's work."

"I agree." D.C. said. "And that brings us back to Shalnokov. He's the one who's had the Rubinov for the last ten years."

Chance tapped a finger on the second file folder. "This is what we've found out about him. When I called him this morning, I had to bulldoze my way through his personal assistant, Regina Meyers. She's very protective of him."

"How did he take the news?" Fiona asked.

"I'd describe his reaction as stoic. Polite even. No sign of shock or outrage that he'd nearly lost his Rubinov."

"Maybe he wasn't surprised," D.C. said. "There's still a possibility that he's somehow connected to the attempted robbery. What's your take on him, Chance?"

"I only met him once, briefly, about five years ago. He wanted to take out insurance with my company. We have a strict policy that we meet prospective clients in person. That was a couple of years before he put the necklace up for auction at Christie's and upped the amount. Basically, I agree with everything in the file. Gregory Shalnokov is a rich eccentric who has the money to create his own world, his own rules."

"And if someone interferes with that?" D.C. asked.

"In my experience, people like Shalnokov don't deal well with interference. He won't agree to see either one of us. He insists that any business we have can be handled by Dr. Meyers. She takes care of everything for him now. I'm meeting with her tomorrow morning to discuss transporting the Rubinov back to his collection after the exhibition closes."

"I talked briefly with her at the National Gallery this morning just before I talked with Charity Watkins," Fiona said. "They seemed to be having a disagreement. I couldn't catch what it was about."

"Maybe I can find out tomorrow," Chance said. "I've also been checking into Arthur Franks. The warden at the Cumberland Security facility was very helpful. Franks has been there three years, and he's been a model citizen. It turns out that the only visitor he's had, except for the FBI, of course, was his great-niece Amanda. She came by in October, shortly after the initial press releases on the upcoming Rubinov exhibition first started."

"No one else has visited him?" Fiona asked.

Chance shook his head. "Franks is very picky about the people he sees. The warden couldn't get him to see me."

Fiona's brows shot up. "He has the right to refuse visitors?"

"That's part of the deal he made with the FBI. In return

for some pretty cushy accommodations in a minimum-security prison and a final say on who he talks to outside of the FBI, he's consulting on major thefts here and in other countries."

"Shades of *Silence of the Lambs,*" D.C. mused. "Only in that movie, the FBI tried consulting with a serial killer."

Chance smiled. "With mixed results. They eventually got their man, but Hannibal Lector turned the whole scenario to his own advantage and escaped."

Fiona tapped her fingers on the table. "Reality is often stranger than fiction. Perhaps Arthur Franks also offered consulting services to his great-niece and his grandson so they could rob the National Gallery."

"Setting up that kind of operation would be next to impossible in one visit," D.C. said.

"Perhaps he isn't the mastermind. What if they just asked him to troubleshoot their plan?" Fiona turned to Chance. "Any phone calls?"

"I checked," Chance said. "Franks doesn't make them."

"E-mails?" Fiona pressed.

Chance shook his head. "He doesn't even have an account. But I did learn one thing from the warden. Franks has developed a hobby. When he isn't consulting for the FBI and Interpol, he's taken up oil painting." Chance ran his hands through his hair. "I talked to someone I know at the FBI, and she says that they're not even asking him about the Rubinov."

"Because the theft was unsuccessful," D.C. said.

"Correct. I thought of asking her to pull some strings to convince Franks to see you, but I wanted to check it out with you two first."

Angling a chair, D.C. sank into it and stretched out his legs. "If he won't talk to an insurance investigator, he'll be even less enthusiastic about talking to a couple of cops. The question is who *would* he talk to?"

Chance's smile widened. "Exactly."

Fiona caught the look Chance exchanged with D.C. "What?"

"Just a little masquerade," D.C. explained.

Fiona frowned. "What kind of a masquerade?"

D.C. continued to look at Chance. "We'd have to appeal to his ego. I'm assuming that it's supersize."

"Safe guess," Chance replied.

"What if a local gallery owner has heard about his painting and is keen on giving him a showing?" D.C. tilted his head in Fiona's direction. "The owner would even bring an art professor along to give her opinion on the work. Once we're there, it would be only natural for us to bring up the attempted robbery and ask his take on it."

"Wait. Time-out," Fiona said. "If Franks has become a recluse and no one knows about his hobby, how would an art gallery get wind of it?"

"She has a point," Natalie said.

"It would have to be through Amanda Hemmings," Fiona said. And then she could have bitten her tongue. She was actually contributing to the crazy ideas being tossed around. Even worse, she was beginning to like them. "But she doesn't have an obvious connection to an art gallery."

"True," D.C. said.

For a moment neither of them said anything. Fiona saw the idea come to D.C. at the same instant it came to her. They spoke in unison. "General Eddinger."

"Amanda could easily have talked to her boss about her great-uncle's hobby," Fiona said.

"And with her connections, General Eddinger could have made contact with a gallery owner," D.C. finished.

"So if he asks, we have an explanation," Fiona said. "And perhaps, because we're using Amanda's visit as a catalyst, he'll talk about the Rubinov."

"I like the way your mind works, Lieutenant."

"I like the way both of your minds work," Chance said.

"It's only a plan," Fiona cautioned. "Franks may not go along with it."

"True," D.C. said. "But I'm betting his ego will tempt him to bite." He shifted his gaze to Chance. "We'll need to lay the ground work before you call the warden."

As Fiona watched, D.C. took out his notebook and began to list items. "We need a real gallery and a real art professor."

"I can handle those," Natalie said. "My sister Sierra teaches at Georgetown and she has a close colleague in the art department. A woman. And there's an art gallery two doors down from the Blue Pepper." Her eyes met her husband's. "Chance and I met there for the first time. The latest owner is a man. I can contact both of them."

"We'll have to get your faces on their Web sites," Chance said. "Just because Franks doesn't have an e-mail account is no reason to believe that he won't do a little research. If he checks you out, we'll have to make sure you're golden." Chance glanced at his watch. "I'll get on that just as soon as Natalie sets things up. When everything's in place, I'll put a call through to the warden."

Fiona rose as Chance helped Natalie lever herself up out of her chair. "What if Franks doesn't agree to see us?"

"Then I'll announce to the press that we're arresting Amanda Hemmings, and we'll ask the FBI to get you in as yourselves," Natalie said.

"Not a bad fallback plan, sweetheart," Chance said as he guided Natalie out of the conference room.

11

THE LAST THING FIONA had expected to be doing that night was sitting at the counter in her kitchen watching D.C. prepare dinner. Natalie and Chance had invited them to the Blue Pepper, but D.C. had explained they had prep work to do for the following day.

He was right. If Arthur Franks bought into their charade, they needed to go over the file Chance had given them. What she hadn't imagined was that the D.C.'s idea of "prep" work had to do with food.

As soon as they'd left the station, he'd driven to a market, the kind you shop for groceries in. The trip still had her head spinning a little. He'd bought *three* bags full of food, and had spread it out over every inch of her counters. Who was going to eat all of it?

"How's the wine?"

She took a sip out of the glass he'd poured her and found she enjoyed the tart, dry taste. "Excellent."

He opened a drawer, selected a knife and peeled an onion. "That looks like a lot of work. We could have ordered in."

"Where's the fun in that?"

She propped her chin on her hand and studied him. "That's really what you do, isn't it? You come up with ideas about having fun." She thought of the way they'd snuck through a hedge and peeked in Kathryn Lewen's window. "That's why you came up with idea of our approaching Arthur Franks as an art professor and a gallery owner. Because it would be more fun?"

"The fun's a side benefit. Although it shouldn't be discounted. Don't you think that if you enjoy your work, you do a better job?"

"I do. But I don't usually think up elaborate masquerades to get it done."

He lifted tomatoes out of a bag and lined them up on the counter. "Police work is often repetitious and tedious. Not only does a bit of a masquerade relieve the boredom, but I always find out something I didn't know before."

"You've done it a lot?"

He took another sip of wine and his eyes twinkled when they met hers. "As often as I can. In Iraq, I was always able to dig up inside information when I wasn't 'Captain D. C. Campbell.'" He set down his glass and selected a tomato. "No matter what approach we take with Franks, he's not going to confess anything."

"Agreed."

"And if we have to put pressure on him through the FBI to see us as two cops, he'll probably be even less cooperative."

She couldn't argue with that, either.

"If Chance can set it up, I believe our little masquerade is the only way we're going to learn anything. Franks will have his guard down. And we'll be appealing to his ego." He paused as he began to chop a tomato. "I know you agree with me. You wouldn't have gone along with the plan otherwise."

He saw so much, Fiona reminded herself. What she couldn't quite admit or understand was that she was looking forward to the undercover work. *If* Franks bought into their story.

D.C. formed the chopped tomatoes into a pile, then set down the knife.

"Is there something you want me to do to help?"

"Put some music on."

She moved to her CD player. "Do you have any preferences? I lean toward the classical."

"Lean away."

He glanced up as the first notes floated out from the speakers. "'Pachabel's Canon.' That will do nicely."

She stared at him.

As if he could feel her gaze, he glanced at her. "You're wondering how it is that I like Baroque music?"

"A little." She climbed back on her stool and studied him as he washed a mound of greens and wrapped them in a paper towel.

"My father had a huge collection, going back to phonograph records. He liked all kinds of music—jazz, blues, classical. After he died, my mother used to listen to it a lot. She told us it was a way of remembering him. So I like them all, too, depending on my mood. What else do you lean toward besides classical?"

She narrowed her eyes. "All of the above plus show tunes. This is more date talk, isn't it?"

He grinned and raised one of his hands, palm outward. "Busted again."

She couldn't prevent a smile, nor could she stop herself from relaxing a little. She toed off her boots and watched as he tore the greens he'd washed into a salad bowl. It amazed her how easily he made the transition from partner to lover to friend to…gourmet chef? He was certainly good at the chopping-things-up part.

He pulled a brand sticker off the bottom of a pot, rinsed it out, and filled it with water. "You don't cook much."

"I don't cook at all. Natalie and Chance gave me the pans as a housewarming gift when I moved in here."

He set the pot over a flame. "Too bad. Fixing a meal is one of the two best ways I know to relax and recharge after a busy day."

"And the other one?"

He lifted his wineglass and held her gaze over the rim. What she saw in his eyes had her skin vibrating in a shock wave of little explosions. Her toes curled on the rung of the chair. "Oh."

"We'll get to that."

And they would. The knowledge, the certainty of the fact that they would make love again had been humming between them all day like an electric current, sometimes with more intensity, other times with less. She felt it surge as her gaze drifted to his hands. His fingers were long, his movements quick and competent.

He'd been just as skilled when he'd touched her bare skin. She wanted to touch him, too. There'd been no time for exploration in Amanda's apartment. All she'd had was a sample of how those hard muscles felt beneath her palms.

They reached for their wine at the same time, sipped and set the glasses down. The current spiked through her veins again as she met his eyes.

"You know what they say about anticipation," he said.

She did. But she'd never before experienced it like this. D.C. was so different for her. No man had ever aroused this level of need in her. No other man had pushed his way this far into her life. She'd known him for little more than twenty-four hours, and here he was—a large man in a black sweater and jeans…filling up her kitchen. And she wanted nothing more than to walk around the counter and drag him to the floor.

Focus, Fiona.

She forced her gaze back to the piles of chopped vegetables. "What are you making?"

"The simplest dish I know. Linguine with fresh tomato and basil sauce."

She ran her gaze over the cluttered counter. "It doesn't look simple."

He laughed. "It is. My mom believed in sitting down with the family at dinner time. Since she worked all day, the recipes couldn't be too complicated. And they had to be fast. Jase and I were always starving. To speed things up, she gave my brother and sister and me the prep jobs." He located a skillet, set it on a burner.

She ran her finger around the rim of the glass. The picture he was painting of a loving family triggered a sudden memory. "My mom died when I was four, my father before that. But I remember she used to chop things, too. She'd let me stand on a chair next to the counter and watch. I haven't thought of that in years."

"The sense of smell can trigger memories."

"One of the foster moms I had used to cook, too. Nothing fancy. Mostly from cans."

He added oil to the skillet. "And the others?"

She shook her head. "Not so much. We had sandwiches a lot. Pizza and fast food when the checks came in." She took another sip of her wine. She didn't usually talk about her past.

"Pizza and fast food. My brother and I would have loved that. To tell you the truth we hated working in the kitchen at first. Not manly enough. But my mother insisted on being an equal opportunity employer."

Fiona thought of the woman she'd met at the skating rink and believed she could grow to like her.

"Once the water boils, we're on a nine-minute timer. So we can squeeze in a little more date talk." He leaned his hip against the counter and picked up his glass. "Why don't you ask me a question? There's got to be something about me you're still curious about."

She was, but she hadn't allowed herself to ask before. There was something about having a man making a mess in her kitchen that undermined her defenses. "Your leg. What happened?"

"I was finishing up my last deployment in Iraq. A shop owner had been under surveillance. He was under suspicion for supplying insurgents with guns. My partner received a call from an informant telling us that he could give us proof—that a deal was going down right then. We had parked down the block, and the bomb went off just as we reached the shop. Perfect timing. David was killed and my leg took some collateral damage. I had a lot of time to think about it when I was lying around in hospitals."

Something tightened inside of Fiona. "You played the blame game." She'd done the same thing after her partner had taken a bullet in that alley. At least she'd had the job to come back to. D.C. hadn't.

She imagined what it might have been like to have nothing to do but stare up at a hospital ceiling and think about all the could haves and should haves…

The image had her sliding off the stool and joining him on the other side of the counter. She slipped her arms around him and felt his wrap around her. Then she simply held on. "I'm sorry. I didn't mean to open that up for you."

"It's all right."

When he ran a hand down her hair, it seemed the most natural thing in the world for her to lay her cheek against his chest. For moments the silence stretched between them, marred only by music and the hiss of a flame beneath a pot. Though she knew she should, she didn't want to move.

"How did you get past it?" she murmured.

"By finally remembering what my father used to say. Omniscience doesn't come with the uniform. That goes for cops, too."

"Yes." Something she hadn't been aware of eased inside of her. She continued to hold on to him, baffled by her need to comfort. To be comforted?

This time it wasn't the snap and sizzle of desire that she felt, but something warmer and sweeter. Everything inside of her tilted, and she recognized it for what it was. Emotion. That was what had her finally pulling away and taking a cautious step back.

Life had taught her that everything was temporary. Wanting more, dreaming of having more had never worked for her.

D.C. leaned a hip against the counter. It was the first time she'd voluntarily touched him. He wasn't sure she was aware of that. He was. Just as he was aware of how right she'd felt in his arms. He wanted to pull her to him again and hold her just like that for hours.

The lieutenant guarded her emotions closely. Even now, she was regrouping, gathering her reserve. When she finally met his eyes, that reserve was as firmly in place as it had been in the sculpture garden when she'd pointed her gun at him.

The temptation to shatter her control flared as bright and hot as the flame under the nearby pot. He wanted very much to grab her and kiss her. But he wouldn't stop with a kiss. And that wasn't the plan. He'd promised himself that tonight they were going to share a meal, and then he was going to seduce her. Slowly.

So when he caught the first sound of the water rolling into a boil, he shifted his attention to the stove and added salt and oil to the pot. "Finally, we're getting somewhere."

"How's your leg now?" she asked.

"On the mend. They had to rebuild it and there's a lot of high tech stuff in there." He patted his thigh. "I was hoping for super powers."

"Leaping over skyscrapers in a single bound?"

"Something like that. Turns out that kind of thing only happens on TV shows. I'll have to be satisfied with around eighty-five percent of the mobility I used to have. The good news is that I'll be able to ditch the cane."

"And the bad news?"

He glanced at her as he picked up a package of linguine. "My general's pushing me to put in for a desk job at the Pentagon."

He saw shock and concern flash into her eyes.

"Are you going to do that?"

He lifted a brow. "Would you take a desk job?"

"Maybe. When I'm sixty."

He laughed. Then taking her by the arms, he lifted her off her feet and twirled her around the small kitchen. "Thanks!"

Fiona's head was still spinning when he set her back down. He kissed first one cheek and then the other, and her head did another spin.

"Thanks for what?"

"Your perspective is just what I needed. I made the right decision last night."

"What did you decide?"

"I'm going to resign from the army on January 15 and seek employment elsewhere."

Fiona simply stared at him.

He turned back to the stove and ignited the flame under the skillet.

"Where?" And why did she care? Why was there a tightening around her heart? A flutter of panic in her stomach?

He shrugged. "My brother would give me a job in Manhattan. Or I could talk to Chance and see if his firm might have a place for me. I'm not sure yet."

"Doesn't it bother you to have to leave the army?"

"I thought it would, but I like the idea of having a clean slate."

Fiona firmly ignored the sinking feeling in her stomach. She didn't want to think that what she and D.C. had right now would end all too soon. She couldn't see the end, but dwelling on it, fearing it, would only spoil the present.

He adjusted the flame under the skillet. "Why don't you get some plates and flatware? Once I put the pasta in the water, we're nine minutes from dining."

For now, he was here. And she'd wasted enough time. Slipping out of her jacket, she dropped it to the floor, then pulled off her belt. "Is there anything there that will spoil if you turn off the burners?"

"Spoil?"

When he turned, she let her slacks drop to the floor and stepped out of them. The linguine box slipped from his hand to the counter with a soft satisfying thud. Power rippled through her.

Without taking his eyes off her, he reached behind him and fumbled once before he extinguished the flames. Then he cleared his throat. "I planned on feeding you first and then seducing you."

"As much as I appreciate a good plan, I have a different proposal to offer." She shrugged out of her blouse and let it drop.

D.C.'s head began to spin, his blood pounding as his eyes moved of their own accord down her body and then slowly up again. Her legs were even longer than he'd imagined. And her skin was pale and delicate-looking, a striking contrast to the strength he'd already discovered. But it was her eyes that grabbed his attention. Was that a hint of mischief he saw?

Surprise shimmered in the wave of heat that moved through him. "Yes, you do."

"I figure if we wait to make love until after we eat, the anticipation might interfere with our enjoyment of the meal. And you've worked so hard on it."

"Logical." But there was very little logic to what he was feeling. To keep from grabbing her and finishing what she'd started, he leaned back against the counter and gripped the edges with his hands.

"One thing though." She pushed her hair back over her shoulders. "It's my turn to take the lead."

"The lead?"

She closed the distance between them and ran one finger down the front of his sweater. "Since I've let you make most of the moves so far, Captain, I thought you might be interested in some of mine."

"Sure." She was weaving a spell around him. He couldn't recall a woman ever doing that before. And the feeling was leaving him weak.

She tapped a finger on his chest. "There are some ground rules."

"You know how I am about rules."

The mischief showed itself again in her smile. "Then we'll keep it simple. You can't touch me until I tell you to. And you have to take off your clothes."

The second one was easy enough. D.C. tugged off his sweater and dropped it to the floor. Then he unfastened his jeans and got rid of them and his shoes. It gave him something to do with his hands besides grab her and pull her to the floor. Or lift her onto a counter. The image of doing that and sinking into her teased at the edge of his mind until she stepped back just out of reach.

When she ran her gaze up and down his body, he felt the heat as intensely as if she'd touched him. An edgy ache began to build inside of him.

"I like your hands." In a quick move, she captured one of them, meeting his eyes as she kissed each one of his fingers. Ice and fire raced along his nerve endings.

"They're strong. Hard. I was watching them while you were chopping things up, and I was wondering…"

D.C. found he had to clear his throat. "Wondering what?"

"How they might feel on my skin."

"Say the word."

"Soon." Linking her fingers with his, she took his other hand, this time pressing her lips to his palm.

"Then there's your mouth. I like that, too. It's clever. Skilled. Every time you kiss me, I can't think of anything but you." Keeping his hands loosely clasped in hers, she rose to her toes and brushed her lips over his.

He leaned forward, capturing her mouth and deepening the kiss until his mind clouded with her taste. Her quiet sigh raced through him. But then she pulled back.

"I could go on kissing you for hours."

"I'm game." He was surprised to hear the hoarseness in his voice.

"Soon." She nipped his bottom lip and whispered, "Soon."

The words sent a shock wave of heat through him. Though she still had his hands in hers, they both knew that he could easily break free. She was deliberately trying to make him lose control. Realizing that was the only thing that allowed him to keep a slim grip on his sanity. "I'm going to have you."

"Of course." Her tone was maddeningly amiable. "But remember the rules. First, I'm going to touch you. You didn't let me touch you at all this morning."

Releasing him, she ran her hands from his waist up his rib cage. Slowly. The gentle brush of her fingers over his nipples tore at what was left of his restraint, and rationality began to slip away as she took one and then the other into her mouth.

She drew back, met his eyes and said, "Now."

D.C. yanked her to the floor.

Triumphant, Fiona gloried in what she'd started. She knew exactly what he was feeling as his hands raced over her, molding, bruising. She felt it, too—a savage, consuming hunger. It raged through her system, blocking out everything. With her hands tangled in his hair, her body on fire, she thought only of him. There were no yesterdays, no tomorrows. Just D.C. and what they could bring each other.

His taste filled her—all those dark, forbidden flavors, but there was no time to savor them, not when her need was so huge. Desperate, she rolled him over so that she could lie along the length of him. Now his hardness was pressed against her, but it wasn't close enough. When his mouth freed hers briefly, she bit his shoulder. "I said now."

He couldn't breathe, couldn't think. Couldn't get enough of her. Pulling her beneath him, he ran his hands over her again. Her skin was silky, hot, irresistible—smooth here, firm there. Each texture burned through him and sharpened the ache inside of him. With his lungs burning, he took his mouth on the same quick journey his hands had taken. He found pleasure, hot and molten at her breasts, sweet and pungent along her rib cage, her narrow waist. Still, it wasn't enough.

Moving his mouth lower, he found the liquid heat at her center. Only then did he linger, slipping his hands beneath her and gripping her tightly while he feasted. And feasted. Her flavors flowed into him until they filled him completely. When she arched against him, gasping his name, he felt himself slip to the edge of reason. Teetering there, he tarried until he felt the next shock of pleasure sweep through her.

Then breathless, his need almost unbearable, he managed to get the condom from his discarded jeans and fumble it into place. Finally, he settled his body over hers. Inches away he stared into her eyes and saw himself. He was hers.

You're mine.

He wasn't sure who said the words, but they drove him to take her with a force that had her choking out his name. He covered her mouth with his and swallowed the sound. Then he could hear nothing but the roar of his own blood, feel nothing but unspeakable pleasure as he drove her and she drove him until there was no one and nothing but blinding heat, swirling colors and the two of them.

This was all he wanted. Everything he wanted. Caught up in her and the storm they were creating, they both moved faster and faster until they broke free together.

12

IT WAS NEARLY TEN when Fiona twisted the last of her linguine around her fork.

"More?" D.C. asked.

She waved a hand. "No. It was wonderful. I'll be lucky if I can get up after this."

"We don't have to." He smiled at her over the rim of his wineglass.

"Give me a few minutes and you're on."

He threw back his head and laughed. When she joined him, D.C. had to suppress the urge to pull her onto his lap and make love to her again. She didn't laugh nearly often enough.

They were sitting like little kids on the floor of her living room. It had taken them a long time to get to dinner. In D.C.'s opinion, it was a long, delicious time. After they'd made love on her kitchen floor, he'd taken the lead by carrying her into the shower. Then while they were dressing, she'd shoved him onto the bed, and they'd made love again.

The move had surprised him. Entranced him. He knew that everything was happening very fast between them. The war had gotten him used to expecting fast changes. Adjusting to them was the key to survival. But Fiona didn't come from a battlefield—at least not the same type he'd experienced. He thought of what she'd said that morning—about the temporary nature of their relationship, and something akin to fear tightened inside of him.

She'd opened up to him for the first time earlier, sharing what had passed for cooking in some of the foster homes she'd lived in. He'd had a tough enough time accepting the loss of his father when he'd been nine, but he couldn't imagine what it might have been like to lose both parents at the age of four. He wanted to ask. He eventually would. But for now he didn't want to spoil her mood.

Instead he said, "You don't like Christmas."

"It's pretty obvious, isn't it?" She reached for her wineglass and twirled the stem in her fingers. "I don't have a tree. I don't have any funny stories to share about wrapping and hiding presents. Last night, when I was on the way to the Blue Pepper, I was even praying for some kind of crime to occur so that I could get out of going to Natalie's party."

"I was praying for the same thing. Boredom was my excuse."

For a moment, neither of them spoke. D.C. let the time spin out. As an interrogator, he'd learned that crucial questions were often answered to fill a silence.

With a sigh, Fiona set her glass down, then drew her knees up to wrap her arms around them. "I stopped believing in Santa Claus when I was adopted."

"Why?"

"They had two children of their own. The boy was twelve, the girl ten. They were busy with school and their friends most of the time. The adoption was the mother's idea. I think she missed having a little one around the house. No one else in the family wanted me there. Especially not the two kids. They thought it was funny to get me into trouble. They'd lie about things I'd done. I wasn't quite five yet, and not even the mother believed me when I would deny things."

She was staring into a space that he couldn't see. All he could do was set his wineglass down and put his arm around her.

"One day near Christmas, the two kids took crayons, scribbled all over the dining-room walls and told their mother that they'd caught me red-handed. I denied it, but I was the outsider. The father thought I should learn a lesson, so there were no presents for me under the tree on Christmas morning. I had to sit there and watch while everyone else opened theirs."

In spite of the fury that flared to life inside of him, D.C. kept his voice even. "What happened then?"

"When I cried, I was sent to my room and told that was what Santa did to bad girls. A few days later I was returned to foster care."

Once again, D.C. banked his anger. "So it was a double whammy. Not only did Santa punish you for being bad, but the mother gave up the battle and rejected you, too."

"Yes." The word came out on another sigh as she settled her head on his shoulder.

D.C. drew her closer. "No wonder you don't have a tree."

She lifted her head to study him in that careful way she had. "Most people don't understand."

He traced a finger along her jaw. "That's not all, is it? What else happened to you at Christmas?"

"You see a lot."

"I'm a cop."

She dropped her gaze. "You'll laugh."

He tilted up her chin and met her eyes. "No."

"I fell in love for the first time at Christmas."

There was suddenly a harsh metallic taste in his mouth. Jealousy? "Tell me."

"It's a really old and corny story."

"My favorite kind."

"I was sixteen and he was captain of the football team at the high school I was attending."

D.C. tightened his grip on her. "Go on."

"Do you remember your first love?"

"Mandy Reardon."

"Shawn Hancock. He'd gone out with lots of girls before me, but I didn't think of that. I was so blindsided by his attention I got stars in my eyes. He was the first thing I thought of in the morning, the last thing I thought of at night."

D.C. swallowed and tasted metal again.

"He took me to movies, let me wear his football sweater. No one had ever paid me that much attention before. I fell so hard. And I didn't ask any questions. Maybe, I didn't want the answers."

D.C. wanted to get up and pace. He wanted to break something. But that wasn't what she needed. He eased her head back onto his shoulder.

After a moment, she continued. "It was just two days before Christmas when he asked for his sweater back. He needed it to give to his next girlfriend. I was so stupid."

"No. You were sixteen and you'd fallen in love for the first time. And he was a class-A jerk."

He felt her smile against his shoulder, and something inside of him eased. "I'm not going to hurt you, Fiona."

"You said that before. And you won't mean to. I know that. I'm not stupid enough to mix you up with Shawn."

D.C. wanted to argue. But words weren't going to work with her. And not everything could be settled with logic and language. He would just have to show her.

"Do you know the best way to develop a different attitude toward Christmas?"

She lifted her head to meet his eyes. "I'm sure you're going to tell me."

"Build new memories. I could help with that."

She read his intention and felt her own immediate response. "By all means." When she reached for him in invitation, all he did was frame her face in his hands.

"My lead this time." Then his mouth brushed against hers lightly, once and then twice, as if he were savoring some new delicacy.

He didn't touch her, not in the hard, hungry ways he'd done before. His hands remained on her face, but the pressure was light, as if she were a fragile piece of glass. She wasn't. She should tell him that, but she didn't want him to stop. He'd never kissed her this way before. No one had. His tenderness weakened her, blurring her thoughts and melting her muscles.

And still he continued to kiss her and kiss her. Time spun out as the whole world narrowed to the brush of his tongue, the nip of his teeth, and the seemingly infinite number of ways his mouth could meld with hers. He was taking her someplace she'd never been. But any fear she might have felt faded in the onslaught of pleasure. Even when his hands left her face to untie her robe and lower her to the carpet, his lips continued to caress her, soft, moist and so patient.

She felt him shrug out of his own clothes, heard him deal with the condom, and when he finally settled over her, she would have clasped him to her and demanded more, but her arms had grown so heavy.

"Look at me, Fiona."

When she did, he continued, "I'm going to touch you, and I want to see what you feel when I touch you."

With his fingertips only, he traced her shoulder blades and

the length of her arms. Like his kisses, the caresses were featherlight. Sensation layered over sensation as his hands stroked and stroked. She'd felt his strength before and gloried in his demands. But this was different, and it was more than heat and passion that filled her. There was something in his eyes—something that had emotion welling up in her until it burned her throat.

"I want you, Fiona."

"I know... You can..."

"I will." He leaned down and touched his mouth to hers softly as his hands moved lower. And lower.

"I will have you." The words were a promise, and as if to fulfill it, he slipped two fingers into her and began to stroke. This time the excitement built in a way it never had before. She felt as if she were caught up in a wave of pleasure that lifted her higher and higher.

She arched up, and as if he were waiting for that signal, he withdrew his hand and filled her. Still he moved slowly, taking her gently up the wave and keeping them on the crest. Lost in the world he had created for her, she matched his rhythm and they moved as one.

D.C. dug for control. This was what he'd wanted—to give her everything. But he hadn't known that her surrender would take him beyond anything he'd experienced before. When she arched up against him and shuddered, he felt the power whip through him. But still he leashed it. His muscles trembled as the blood pounded at the back of his neck.

He had to taste her again. Her lips softened, gave, and filled him with a sweet, dark ache.

"Fiona."

She opened her eyes.

"Come with me."

"Yes." Her hands found and gripped his, holding firm as they climbed together toward the next peak and flew over.

THE PHONE WOKE FIONA. When her eyes flew open, she found she was staring into D.C.'s. They were lying facing each other on the couch in her living room, and she couldn't recall quite how they'd gotten there.

As bits and pieces returned, he reached over his head, lifted the handset of the phone and glanced at the caller ID.

"It's Natalie," he said as he clicked it on and held it so they both could hear.

At first, she thought that the baby might have come early. "Natalie?"

"Turn on your TV. Eleven o'clock news. Channel 5."

D.C. rolled up to a sitting position, clicked her set on with the remote and punched in the channel. She sat up next to him and kept the receiver between them.

Breaking News flashed in a red banner headline at the bottom of the screen. *Prime suspect identified in Rubinov Diamond Case—Private Amanda Hemmings.* A local news reporter, Mariah Evans, stood outside the hospital where Fiona and D.C. had visited Amanda Hemmings.

"You decided to leak it?" Fiona asked.

"No. It's either crackerjack investigating by our local news star, or Mariah has a source who knows a lot about the case. She's reported that Amanda Hemmings was found in the sculpture garden with the necklace on her. And Mariah's also uncovered Amanda's connection to Arthur Franks," Natalie said. "I'm expecting a call from the commissioner who will press for an arrest. I'll hold off until you can interview Hemmings again tomorrow morning. In the meantime, I'm sending two more uniforms to make sure the press doesn't get in to see her."

On the TV, the scene shifted to a clip of Natalie's press conference that morning, and Fiona saw her own face flash on the screen. Mariah was informing her audience that the police investigation headed up by Lieutenant Fiona Gallagher had reported no progress as of yet on the case.

"Natalie?" D.C. said.

"D.C., I'm glad you're there, it'll save me a phone call. Can you make sure General Eddinger knows about this latest development?"

"I will," D.C. said.

"On the bright side, Chance thinks that this news will tempt Arthur Franks to take the bait and agree to see the two of you tomorrow. Your identities are all set up, and he made arrangements with the warden earlier this evening."

"I'm on the same wavelength as your husband on that. It won't be just ego pulling him in. If he had any kind of a connection at all with his great-niece, he'll want to talk to someone who knows her. And if he suspects that she had anything at all to do with the attempted robbery, he won't want to talk to the police."

There was a ring in the background.

"That will be the commissioner. I'll contact you in the morning."

Fiona had no sooner hung up the phone than D.C. grabbed her hands and pulled her to her feet. "Work or play?"

"What?"

"Do you want to study our backgrounds in case we get the chance to visit Franks tomorrow or do you want to go another round?"

"Work," she said. "I think we've played enough tonight." But, Lord, she was tempted to just push him back down on the couch. Her work had always come first, and they had a full day tomorrow. How had she changed so much in such a short time?

He leaned down and brushed his lips against hers. "Not nearly enough. But we'll do some prep work first."

Her eyes narrowed on his. "Not more cooking."

He grinned at her. "I'm talking about the file on Arthur Franks. We're going to have to be very convincing if we intend to fool him."

The next morning, D.C. waited on the other side of a glass wall looking into Amanda Hemmings's hospital room. A short distance away, a uniformed officer stood guard. Another uniform stood near the nurses' station. Fiona had checked and no one had been allowed in to visit Amanda since the last time they'd been there. And Billy Franks hadn't been back.

So Amanda and Billy hadn't had a chance to communicate or get their stories straight. If they had a story.

Through the glass, he could see Amanda sitting up in a chair. The IV tubes were gone, and some of the bandages had been removed. Physically, she was making progress. General Eddinger and Dr. Laura Whitmore, the psychiatrist Eddinger had hired, stood near the foot of the bed. The trio had left the door ajar so that he could hear what was being said.

Dr. Whitmore introduced Amanda to her visitors. While she went on to explain why they were there, D.C. studied the young woman. She might be up and ambulatory, but she was clasping her hands together so tightly that her knuckles had turned white.

When General Eddinger began to speak, her motherly tone had Amanda's hands relaxing a bit. He and Fiona had discussed their strategy briefly on their way over in the car. He'd agreed that she take the lead on this one. Taking turns had worked for them so far, and this way he got to read Amanda's body language. Besides, if they got in to see Arthur Franks, it would be his turn to be in charge.

Chance had personally delivered the copy of the Rubinov necklace earlier to Fiona's apartment. He hadn't heard anything from the warden yet, nor had he gotten any leads on who might have made the copy.

Inside the room, Fiona pulled a chair up next to Amanda's and sat down.

"AMANDA," FIONA BEGAN, "General Eddinger and I are here to ask you if you remember anything about how you ended up in the hospital."

Amanda shifted her gaze to Dr. Whitmore.

The doctor nodded. "Tell them what you told me."

Amanda glanced back at Fiona. "I can't remember anything before I woke up here. It's a blank."

Dr. Whitmore had already filled them in on that much. But Fiona had wanted to hear it from Amanda. Either the young woman was a very skilled actress, or she'd really lost her memory. And the sympathy Fiona felt for her wasn't helping her to ascertain which. She succeeded in pushing her feelings away, but she couldn't prevent herself from placing a hand over Amanda's.

"I've explained to Ms. Hemmings that her amnesia is most probably temporary, and that with the proper time and rest, it should start to come back to her," Dr. Whitmore added.

But time was running out. The media was already camped out in front of the hospital. If it hadn't been for D.C.'s quick decision to go in through the emergency room entrance, she would have been peppered with questions about how soon an arrest would be made. And the answer to that, she was very much afraid, was soon.

"Amanda, I want to show you something to see if it stirs up a memory. Is that okay with you?"

"Sure."

Fiona didn't miss the hope that leaped into the young woman's eyes.

"I'll do anything if it will help me remember."

Something in her voice brought back the memory of the first time Amanda had walked into her office—young and eager, so excited at the prospect of doing something for the families of the Walter Reed patients. And for the first time, Fiona didn't blame herself for feeling sympathetic to Amanda's situation. Her cop's instinct was telling her that the young woman hadn't been in on the theft.

Fiona reached into her purse, drew out the copy of the Rubinov necklace and held it up to the light.

"No." Amanda's eyes went wide with fright, and Fiona could have sworn that she was seeing something beyond the necklace.

"He's in danger…" The anxiety in her tone sharpened. "Have to…do something…stop him."

"Amanda." Dr. Whitmore's voice was soothing.

Fiona held up her free hand to stop her. "Amanda, what else do you remember?"

"Eliminate him…that's what she said."

"Who?" Fiona pressed.

Then she watched as Amanda's eyes rolled back in her head and closed.

"That's all." Dr. Whitmore spoke in a clipped tone as she circled the bed. "I must ask you to leave, and I won't allow any more questions today."

Heart aching, Fiona tucked the necklace into her purse and followed General Eddinger out of the room.

"Good work, Lieutenant," D.C. said as they moved

toward the elevators. "You've opened a door. She's starting to remember."

"It was your idea to bring the necklace," Fiona returned.

"Very good work by both of you, then," Eddinger said. "That young woman isn't a thief. Whatever her involvement, her goal wasn't to steal the Rubinov."

"I agree," Fiona said. "But we don't have enough to prove that yet. We need to know who *he* is and who *she* is. I'm favoring her cousin Billy Franks for the he. He and his pals are in on this somehow. But my boss is going to need more than what Amanda gave us to keep the commissioner from insisting on an arrest."

"Then I'll just have to have a chat with the commissioner." General Eddinger led the way out of the elevator. "The two of you should leave through another exit. I'll talk with the press a bit."

They were just exiting the hospital when D.C. checked his phone. "Chance called," he said as he punched in numbers. After a moment, he grinned at her. "We've got the go-ahead from the warden to visit Arthur Franks."

13

THE WINDOWLESS ROOM the warden placed them in reminded
D.C. of an army mess hall. Rows of tables and chairs filled
the center of the room and vending machines lined one wall.

"This isn't like the movies," Fiona said. "I was thinking he'd
be behind glass and we'd have to talk to him through a phone."

"They're not housing any violent criminals here," D.C.
said as he adjusted her glasses. "So they keep it more relaxed.
Are you ready to play your part?"

"I don't have much of a part to play." She glanced down at
the clothes that Chance had provided. "Seems to me all I
have to do is look like a frump while you take the lead."

He studied her for a moment. At his direction, she'd pulled
her hair up into a messy bun with strands hanging out in much
the same way Billy Franks's neighbor had worn hers. The
careless, artistic type. Even with the hair and an oversize pair
of glasses, D.C. didn't believe she quite pulled off frump. But
she was definitely a sharp right turn from the woman who'd
first strode toward him in the sculpture garden. Had it only
been two days ago?

He ran a finger down her nose. "Any more theories on
who Amanda was referring to as *she?*"

He and Fiona had batted around ideas on the ride to the
prison. If the *he* was Billy, the four *shes,* other than Amanda,

who might be linked even somewhat loosely with him or the diamond were Carla Mason, Billy's study pal in the lace-up black boots, Professor Kathryn Lewen, her sister, Charity Watkins and Regina Meyers.

"Kathryn and Charity are still my prime suspects. We can connect the dots between the two of them and Billy and the diamond. But where do Shalnokov and Arthur Franks fit in?"

"Maybe they don't," D.C. said. "Perhaps the two sisters set up the entire operation. Kathryn's got a near genius student who might have the ability to break through the National Gallery's security system. And Charity Watkins sets up the exhibition with Shalnokov and provides inside information."

"But Amanda is the one who ended up with the Rubinov in her pocket. And she's the only one who had any contact with Arthur Franks."

"Speak of the devil," D.C. murmured. The man they'd come to see was walking toward them. Arthur Franks was a small, thin man with a dancer's body. He reminded D.C. a bit of Fred Astaire, an actor who'd danced his way through many a Hollywood film. Ironically enough, the star had also briefly played a thief on a hit TV series.

He and Fiona had read the file on Franks last night, and the man's agility in his earlier years had rivaled Houdini's. He could slip through electronic surveillance as easily as he could scale buildings. D.C. couldn't help but wonder what it might be like to give up something one had such a talent for? Would he ever be able to give up investigative work?

Out of the corner of his eye, he could see that Fiona was studying the man just as closely as he was. What did she see? Odd how much he was coming to depend on her perspective.

"I've got an idea," he murmured.

Fiona stifled a sigh. "I don't know if I want to hear it."

"I'm the one who came up with the idea of the masquerade. So why don't you ask the questions?"

She stared at him. "You're kidding, right?"

"No. You have good instincts. I have a feeling you might get more out of him than I will."

A feeling. Nerves danced in her stomach. She'd been sure that D.C. was going to take the lead on this one. It was his turn. She hadn't bothered to come with a strategy.

"Improvise," D.C. murmured in a voice only she could hear.

Then she pushed all that aside and concentrated on the legendary thief as he reached them. Close up, Arthur Franks had the kind of nondescript face that would fade easily from memory. But the eyes wouldn't. They were bright blue and had a twinkle in them that held pure amusement.

What was so funny? she wondered.

Reaching across the table, Franks held out his hand to Fiona first.

She shook it. "I'm Diane Lincoln. I teach in the art department at Georgetown."

His chuckle held warmth. "No, you're not Dr. Lincoln. You're Lieutenant Fiona Gallagher and your picture on TV is much prettier than you are in person. I imagine you must have worked very hard to achieve this dowdy look."

Shit, she thought. But Fiona kept her eyes on Franks. "It took over an hour. What gave me away?"

"The eyes. They're hard to disguise even behind glasses, and yours are very distinctive. I always used to have trouble with mine."

He offered his hand to D.C. "Are you indeed Gabriel Martin, the gallery owner my niece contacted?"

"No." D.C. shook hands. "I'm Captain D. C. Campbell. I run the Military Police Unit at Fort McNair."

"Where Amanda was stationed."

D.C. nodded. "You weren't really expecting Diane Lincoln or Gabriel Martin, were you?"

His eyes brows shot up. "Suddenly a gallery owner and an art dealer want to see me a few days after someone tries to steal the Rubinov necklace out of the National Gallery? You should never try to con a con."

Fiona kept her eyes on Arthur Franks. "If we'd asked to come and talk to you as ourselves, would you have seen us?"

"Perhaps. But I don't like my painting time interrupted. It blocks my flow, sometimes for hours. My arrangement with the FBI is very specific. They can only ask me about thefts that have actually occurred—not ones that have been unsuccessful or ones they're anticipating. Otherwise they'd be here all the time."

He waved a hand gesturing them to sit down as he took the chair across from them. "Your more creative approach intrigued me. Plus, I just finished a painting yesterday. So your timing was good."

And Fiona's instinct told her that he was curious. He wanted information as much as they did. She leaned toward him. "That's not the only reason you agreed to see us. You're worried about your Amanda."

"Perhaps. Based on the news report, it sounds like you're trying to pin this on her."

"She's involved in some way," Fiona said.

"But you haven't arrested her. What has she told you?"

Fiona debated a moment. If she told him about the amnesia and he was involved, he'd have the upper hand. But she thought she saw a glimmer of true concern in those blue eyes, so she said, "Nothing. Amanda suffered a blow to the head, and she has amnesia. Temporary, the doctor believes."

Absorbing the news, he leaned back in his chair and folded his hands behind his head. "The newscast said that she was found in the sculpture garden with the Rubinov in her pocket. That, and the fact that she's related to me, makes her a prime suspect. And now you're telling me she can't defend herself because she can't remember."

"Correct."

"She didn't steal it."

"Which, of course, means that you're not involved, either," Fiona said.

He laughed, and the rich, ripe sound of it nearly filled the room. He met D.C.'s eyes first and then Fiona's. "If I'd been involved in any way, you wouldn't have recovered the diamond. And I certainly wouldn't have involved my niece. She's a true innocent."

"Do you have any idea who might have stolen it?" Fiona asked.

Franks shook his head. "I don't have a clue. Let me tell you what I do know. My sister cut herself off from me the first time she learned what I did for a living. She was very religious and didn't want her family to be tainted by my lifestyle. Nor did she want her daughter to be looking up to me as some kind of hero. My son never forgave his aunt, and later when Amanda was orphaned, he refused to take her in—even though by that time, he'd also pretty much cut himself off from me. My sense is that Amanda inherited her grandmother's prim and proper, straight-arrow ways. But she doesn't condemn me for my former profession."

"Why did she come to see you?" D.C. asked.

Franks smiled. "She wanted contact with family. She told me a little of her background. I think her foster home experience left some scars."

"Did she tell you that she'd also contacted your grandson Billy?" Fiona asked.

"She did. She filled me in on where he was, what he was doing. 'Boy genius' was the way she described him."

Fiona didn't miss the hint of pride in his voice. "Have you had any contact with Billy?"

Franks's expression sobered. "You think Billy might be involved also?"

"Yes. He and two college pals," Fiona said. "But we don't think they could have pulled it off alone."

"Maybe. Maybe not. I really have no way of knowing."

He was going to clam up now, Fiona thought. Now that they'd satisfied his curiosity. But she believed he did care for Amanda. She was the one he'd met. She leaned forward. "Look, maybe you're not involved in this. But your blood relatives are. And we think someone is using them. Someone who may have known about their connection with you. What you haven't seen in the news coverage is that they left a very good copy of the necklace in the display case."

Franks gave a long, low whistle. "Then Billy and Amanda definitely weren't in it alone. I don't know my grandson. Haven't seen him since he was a toddler. After his marriage, my son also became worried about whether or not his offspring might try to emulate me. I was asked to keep my distance."

"Maybe that's what Billy was trying to do—emulate you," Fiona said.

Franks considered that, too. And for the first time since he'd sat down, he frowned. "Look, I had nothing to do with this. You can believe what you want, but I gave up my old ways on the day I was sentenced. Ten years is a long time. I won't be able to do what I did, be what I was when I get out. Time takes a toll on someone in my line of work. And technology advances at nearly the speed of light. I've been in here three years. I'm not sure, even if I wanted to, that I could break into the security system at the National Gallery. Besides, now that I'm painting, I've found a new focus. It's something I will be able to do when I'm finally released."

His eyes twinkled briefly again. "And the occasional puzzle the FBI brings me allows me to keep my wits sharp. I may continue to consult for them even after I'm released. But I don't like the fact that I may have influenced my grandchild or my great-niece to get involved in my old lifestyle. What can I do to help?"

Fiona would have bet her badge that he was being sincere. Of course, she was dealing with a class-A con man. She waited another two beats, giving D.C. a chance to comment or give her some clue as to what his take was.

Franks broke the silence. "Let's try this. There aren't many who could make a high-quality copy of the Rubinov. I could give you some names."

"We'd appreciate that. You've seen the necklace?" Fiona asked.

"Shall we say I had it in my possession for a brief time between owners?"

"When?" Fiona asked.

"About ten years ago."

Just about the time Shalnokov first purchased the Rubinov, Fiona thought.

"You also have to be looking at Shalnokov for this," Franks said. "He could recruit the kind of people who'd get the job done."

There was a lot Arthur Franks wasn't saying. A lot of questions he was raising. Had Franks helped Shalnokov gain possession of the Rubinov?

For now, those questions had to be ignored. Fiona leaned forward in her chair. "If that's true and Shalnokov is behind the robbery, why would he involve a rank amateur like your great-niece? Or your grandson?"

"Shalnokov isn't a stupid man. He must have been persuaded that Billy could do the job. And if something went wrong…" Franks shrugged, "A twenty-year-old kid makes a good fall guy."

Fiona's thoughts returned to what Amanda had said. "Would Shalnokov take steps to eliminate Billy afterward?"

Franks's eyes narrowed and grew hard. "Yes, if Billy proved a threat. Or perhaps if he failed. Shalnokov doesn't like to be disappointed. What can I do to help?"

Fiona glanced at D.C. and he pulled out four photos that he'd located on the Internet while she'd changed into drab clothes. The women in the pictures were Regina Meyers, Kathryn Lewen, Charity Watkins and Carla Mason.

"All of these women have a connection with either the diamond or your grandson. Do you recognize any of them?" she asked.

Franks studied them for a few moments. "There's a family resemblance."

"We know two of them are sisters." Fiona pointed to Watkins and Lewen. "Fraternal twins."

Then Franks tapped a finger on one of the other photos, and when he met her eyes, his were twinkling. "This one, I can tell you something about. I didn't recognize her at first. I thought she looked familiar yesterday when I saw her in the newscast, but the camera didn't stay on her for long. She's Shalnokov's spokesperson, right?"

"Yes," Fiona said. "Dr. Regina Meyers."

"Interesting," Franks murmured as his eyes returned to the

photo. "She's changed the color of her hair and the style. The last time I saw her, it was much lighter."

"When was that?" Fiona asked.

"Ten years ago. She's a jewelry designer who's made some of the best copies I've ever seen. One of them was a copy of the Rubinov."

Fiona studied him for a minute, wondering how much more he would tell them. "Did she make it for you?"

He grinned. "No. I believe the copy was commissioned by Shalnokov. And she wasn't calling herself Regina Meyers then. I knew her as Kate McGowan."

FIONA WAS ENERGIZED as they arrived at her station. Although she and D.C. were banking on the fact that Arthur Franks was playing it straight, Fiona's gut instinct told her he was. And they had something now. Not enough. But if Regina Meyers had made the copy, she was connected in some way. Fiona was getting that tingle she always got when the pieces were about to fall into place on a case. She and D.C. had come up with a plan—one that might give those pieces a shuffle and allow them to re-sort themselves. They just had to get Natalie's and Chance's approval and run it by General Eddinger.

"I'm starved," D.C. said as they started up the stairs to the squad room.

"You're always starved. I'm surprised we didn't hit a drive-through on our way back from Cumberland."

The faint sounds of Christmas music drifted to them on the first landing. But it didn't prepare her for what she saw as they entered the squad room. The place was bursting with people, some in army fatigues, some in uniforms, others not. Here and there she recognized faces of her volunteers. And there seemed to be a slew of teenagers. The offices and interrogations rooms that lined the perimeter of the bull pen were also packed.

And they were all wrapping up toys. Rolls of Christmas paper and ribbon seemed to fill every inch of space. A table at the far end was laden with food—boxes of pizzas, platters of sandwiches, bottled water and soft drinks.

Oh, there was some police work going on here and there. She glimpsed a detective tapping the keys of his computer. But the perp he was interviewing was putting tape on a package.

Through the glass, Fiona spotted General Eddinger in her captain's office tying a bow on a box while Natalie supervised with her feet propped up on a chair. At a nearby conference table, Chance was muscling a large teddy bear into candy-cane-striped wrapping paper.

"What is going—?"

"I thought we'd eat here while you gave your report. But first I have to say hello to my mom and sister. Come with me."

He took her arm and drew her with him, not giving her a choice. She spotted the two women she'd met briefly in the sculpture garden. Frantically, she searched for the names. Nancy. That was his mother. And Darcy was his sister.

Nancy took her hands immediately. "You're doing a good thing here, providing a merry Christmas for the children of the young men who've been wounded in the service of our country. I hope you don't mind that I brought some of the students from my school with me. When D.C. called to explain the situation, I thought you might be able to use the extra hands."

"I can." Fiona's throat grew tight as she glanced around the room. "But I didn't do all this." She turned to D.C. "You did."

"You asked if the army could help. I turned the job over to General Eddinger and made a phone call to my mom. The idea started with you."

Her gaze swept the room again. He'd done all this. For her. In her wildest imagination, she couldn't have pictured the scene in front of her. But *he* had. And he'd made it happen. The squad room had been transformed into Santa's workshop.

And there in the midst of Christmas music, stacks of wrapping paper and more presents than she'd ever seen, she felt her heart go into a free fall.

Nancy Campbell handed D.C. a small bag. "Maddie and Jase are expecting us in Manhattan tomorrow for Christmas Eve." She slid her gaze to Fiona. "We'd like you to join us. Will you be able to get away?"

Fiona's pulse skidded and then went into overdrive. "I don't know— This case—"

"We may have to improvise a bit…" D.C. said.

Nancy rolled her eyes. "*Improvise.* That's his theme song. Always coming up with some idea at the last minute. You're going to have to keep him on a short leash."

"I—" Fiona began.

"I have this feeling that the case will break soon. In the meantime, Fiona has to make a report." D.C. leaned down to kiss his mother's cheek before he drew Fiona with him to Natalie's office.

General Eddinger glanced up from tying the bow. "The baby's coming soon. She doesn't believe me, but I know the signs. Her back aches and she hasn't slept for three days."

"I'm not having this baby until we solve this case," Natalie said.

"Willpower is good," Eddinger said. "But nature is stronger."

Natalie winced and rubbed her back as Chance moved to her chair and placed his hands on her shoulders. "You may have a point, General." Then she turned to Fiona. "Report."

Fiona did.

"So it's possible that Dr. Meyers made the copy that we found in the display case ten years ago—at just about the same time she went to work for Gregory Shalnokov," Natalie summarized. "Tough to believe that's a coincidence."

"My brother is already running a background check on Kate McGowan," D.C. said. "He could have something at any time."

"You want to bring her in for questioning?" Natalie asked.

"D.C. and I have something else we'd like to try first. We need Amanda to remember more," she said. "And we have an idea."

"Don't keep us in suspense," Natalie said.

"Since the Rubinov exhibition ends today, we need to move quickly." Fiona turned to General Eddinger. "Do you think you could convince Dr. Whitmore to let us take Amanda to the National Gallery this afternoon? If just looking at the necklace stirred up memories, going there may be enough to release the floodgates."

"Consider it done," Eddinger said.

"D.C. and I also need to find Billy and talk to him. If we're right about Billy being the *he* Amanda believed was in danger, and if someone is planning to make him the fall guy in this, then he'd be safer in custody. If we tell him that, perhaps he'll cooperate."

Natalie waved a hand. "Go. General Eddinger has all of this under control."

The call came through just as they were walking out the door. Natalie took it and called after them. "There's a fire at Billy Franks's apartment building."

14

SMOKE STUNG THE AIR and billowed upward in black columns as they climbed out of D.C.'s car. Lights from the engines swirled, and Fiona could see two streams of water cross-aimed through broken windows on the second and third floors. One glance confirmed her worst fear. "The window on the second floor. It's got to be Billy's apartment."

"Yes," D.C. murmured as he cleared a path through the by-standers that had gathered. A ladder leaned against the front of the building and she counted two firemen on the roof. Three ambulances and several police cruisers had pulled up behind a string of fire engines. Several people wearing blankets were being treated with oxygen. Others gathered behind barricades and watched.

Fiona found her view blocked when she tried to scan the crowd. "Can you see them?"

"No," D.C. said.

There were two possibilities. She and D.C. had run through them on the drive over. Either Billy and his friends had set the fire in an attempt to destroy any evidence that might connect them to the attempted robbery, or someone—who-ever had masterminded the theft—had decided to get rid of the three young people. Both she and D.C. were favoring the latter.

Fiona flashed her badge for one of the uniforms. "Did everyone get out?"

"Can't say. They've been loading ambulances ever since my partner and I got here." He jerked his head toward another uniformed officer standing near one of the vehicles. "Tully over there was on the scene when I arrived. He and his partner Fortino called it in. According to him, it started with an explosion on the second or third floor. They're taking statements."

"Thanks."

She and D.C. ducked beneath the barricade and strode toward Tully, who was talking to a woman in a blanket. The officer was young, fresh-faced, and scribbling in his notebook. The woman he was talking to turned at their approach and Fiona recognized Wendy Davis.

She flashed her badge at Tully while Wendy aimed a smile at D.C.

"Thought you'd eventually come, Captain," Wendy said.

"You all right?" D.C. asked.

Her brows shot up. "Other than being homeless at Christmas, I'm fine. And lucky, I think." She glanced up at the windows where sooty-faced firemen still aimed their hoses. "It happened fast. I was just telling pretty boy here," she gestured at Tully, "there was this loud noise from above me. Third floor, I think. The explosion was powerful enough to shake the walls and dislodge some of my paintings. I just took my Lorelei here and ran."

At the sound of her name, the cat poked her head out of the blanket.

"What about your neighbors?" D.C. asked.

"Lucky, too, I'd say. Firemen got all three of them out," Wendy said.

Fiona turned to Tully and eased him a few steps away. "What do you know?"

"Three kids—two guys and a girl were in the apartment closest to where the fire started. They're in bad shape, Lieutenant. I overheard one of the medics talking about possible broken bones and severe smoke inhalation. They're loading the last one now."

Signaling D.C. to follow, badge in hand, she strode toward the line of ambulances. A uniformed technician closed the doors on the first one, but not before Fiona caught a glimpse of black boots. Carla. With soot and an oxygen mask covering his face, Fiona only managed to identify Mark because of the red hair. That left Billy. Running now, she reached the last ambulance just as a large African American woman slammed the doors shut.

"I need to talk to Billy Franks, the young man you just loaded into this ambulance.

"You can't." The name on her tag read Rochella Martin.

"Look, Miss Martin, we think that the fire may have been set intentionally and that Billy Franks was the intended victim."

"You still can't talk to him."

Fiona opened her mouth, then shut it when Rochella Martin held up a hand.

"I'm not trying to be difficult. The first reason you can't talk to him is because he's still out. Severe smoke inhalation will do that to you. Reason number two is that until we get him to the hospital and treat him for the smoke inhalation, he'll find it difficult to make any sound at all. And he has other injuries that require immediate attention. Do you need any more reasons or will those suffice?"

"Will he be all right?"

The woman raised an eyebrow. "If you'll let us get him to the hospital."

"What about the other two?" Fiona asked.

"Same reasons. Do I need to give them again?"

"No." Fiona found herself staring at the emergency technician's back and called after her, "Where are you transporting them?"

Over her shoulder, the woman gave her the name of the same hospital Amanda was being kept in. "Try in a couple of hours."

Fiona turned to find D.C. grinning.

"You should have used your charm on her."

"It never worked on my mother when she was in that kind of a mood. You can have Natalie post a guard on them at the hospital, and they'll keep for now."

As Fiona headed back to talk to Tully, she updated Natalie and requested the guards. D.C. angled his way to Wendy Davis. While Tully filled her in on the details of what he knew about the fire—not much—D.C. continued to chat with Billy's neighbor. By the time Natalie had called back to say they could pick Amanda up and take her to the National Gallery within the hour, D.C. was holding the cat and Wendy was studying the photos that they'd showed Arthur Franks of Charity Watkins, Kathryn Lewen, Regina Meyers and Carla Mason.

Fiona studied him—a large man holding a small cat and using his not inconsiderable charm on a witness. They shouldn't have been able to work together—and yet they could. Their styles—so different—seemed to mesh perfectly. D.C. turned his head slightly and met her eyes. She felt the instant connection, the pull, and as she did, the noises around her faded. Her heart went into free fall for the second time. This was the moment she'd remember, she thought giddily. While smoke blocked out the sun and the sound of sirens filled the air, the realization streamed through her. In spite of the barricades

she'd put in place, this was the moment she fell in love with
D. C. Campbell.

"Lieutenant?"

As the sound of D.C.'s voice penetrated her thoughts, Fiona
gathered herself and reached him just as Wendy Davis handed
him back the photos.

"The one I left on top is definitely the one you say is Professor Kathryn Lewen. And the top three are related, right?"

"Why do you think that?" Fiona asked.

"The shape of the eyes is very similar on the two younger
ones. And the older one has the same shaped nose and chin
as the professor. I worked my way through college doing por-
traits. I tend to notice things like that."

"Thank you for your help, Wendy," D.C. said as he handed
her the cat.

This time when his eyes met hers, Fiona could see they
were thinking the same thing. She sent a brief nod to Tully
and then turned to walk with D.C. toward the car.

"Meyers, Watkins and Lewen—they're related," Fiona
said. "I got a hint of it when I saw Kathryn Lewen. There was
something familiar about her that I couldn't quite put my
finger on. But Regina Meyers could be an older sister of
Kathryn and Charity."

"I'm betting she's their mother."

Fiona stopped to stare at him. "And they've been planning
this for ten years."

"Looks like."

"We have enough to bring them in for questioning,"
Fiona said.

"I vote we take Amanda to the exhibition at the National
Gallery first. It's closing in two hours, and the insurance
company will be there to provide security for the diamond's

transportation back to Shalnokov's estate. I'm betting that two out of the three of these women will be there, too. If seeing the Rubinov there brings Amanda's memory back, a lot of our questions will be answered." As D.C. punched numbers into his phone, he shot her a grin. "In the meantime, I'll tell my brother to fast-track the check on Kate McGowan."

FIONA STOOD TO THE RIGHT of Amanda's wheelchair a short distance down the hallway from the exhibition room. From their vantage point, they could see D.C. and one of the guards just outside the doors. Viewers were moving at a steady rate from the exhibition room into the hall.

Chance had called just as they'd arrived to say that he wouldn't be personally present to oversee things. Natalie had gone into labor. Someone else from his company would be heading up the transfer and safe transport of the diamond from the National Gallery to Shalnokov's home. Just as D.C. had expected, Regina Meyers and Charity Watkins would be on hand to witness the transfer.

The plan was to wait until the exhibition room had cleared and then to bring Amanda in to see the room and the diamond. The insurance company's security team would give them a few moments of privacy before bringing Watkins and Meyers in and removing the Rubinov from the case. A glance at her watch told Fiona that they had only a few moments to wait.

So far their trip down Amanda's memory lane had yielded nothing concrete. They'd stopped briefly in the sculpture garden, but there'd been no flashes of remembrance. Little wonder, Fiona thought. Amanda's mind wouldn't have been on the art when she'd dashed in there with the Rubinov. Her fight or flight instinct must have blocked everything else out.

"Why can't I remember?"

"You will when you're ready," Fiona said, feeling a bit helpless.

Amanda's knuckles had gone white where they gripped the arms of the wheelchair, her body was rigid. Fiona's heart went out to her, and she squatted down by the private's side. "The Rubinov diamond has a rich history and legend behind it. Do you remember any of it?"

Amanda met her eyes. "No. What is the legend about?"

"The diamond brings lovers together." As Fiona told the story, she found her glance straying more than once to D.C. At one point his eyes had met hers, and an image slipped into her mind—that night in the sculpture garden when for a moment, they'd both been touching the Rubinov. Was that when it had happened? Was that when she'd fallen in love with him? Or had it been even earlier, when she'd first seen him across the display case?

Fear rippled through her, but this time she didn't shove it away. She was going to learn to deal with it. Just as she was going to learn to deal with loving D.C.

"Do you believe in the legend?" Amanda asked.

Just then, D.C. smiled at her and raised his cane to give her a mock salute. Fiona felt the feelings inside of her settle. "Yes. Yes, I do." And she realized what she wanted to do about it.

As D.C. and the guard disappeared into the exhibition room, she rose. They were going to make sure the room was empty, and then one of them would step into the hall and signal Fiona and Amanda forward.

The elevator doors across from them slid open, and people poured out. A husky female voice said, "Under control. Just a few more minutes."

She recognized the voice instantly, but Fiona's attention was distracted by the fact that Amanda's nails were suddenly digging into her arm. Leaning down, she saw something flicker over the young woman's face. Fear?

"That's her." Amanda's voice was barely audible. Fiona squatted down again.

"That's one of the voices I heard." She was breathing hard and the words poured out in a whispered rush. "I was in the café and they were seated behind me in a booth." Amanda pressed her free hand against her stomach. "It's coming back so fast...I..."

"Take your time," Fiona said.

"Earlier, I'd seen Billy. He was wearing a Santa hat and a scarf like mine. Then I lost him in the crowd, and I ended up in the café. I got some tea."

Fiona caught a glimpse of the two women now. They'd stopped outside the exhibition room. She had no trouble recognizing Charity Watkins and Regina Meyers. The voice Amanda had recognized belonged to one of them.

"She was talking about Billy and what a genius with electronics he was. He was the perfect choice to steal the Rubinov." Amanda spoke quickly. "She said that he'd come by his talent naturally, that his grandfather could be proud of him."

"Did you hear what the other woman said?"

"She kept her voice low. I only caught phrases—*should have kept it in the family...mistake to involve outsiders.* Something about *Kathryn always wanting to keep her hands clean.* The other woman said that there was nothing to worry about. Once they had the diamond, Billy would be eliminated. He would make the perfect fall guy when the theft was eventually discovered."

Ahead of her, Fiona saw the two women enter the room and

she frowned. They were early. She debated following them, but she didn't want to interrupt what Amanda was remembering.

THE RUBINOV DIAMOND seemed to pulse with life as D.C. reached the display case. "It's a damn shame that it's going back into someone's vault," he murmured.

"I'll second that," Bobby said. "But perhaps it's done its work for a while. I understand that the number of June weddings booked in Washington and the outlying areas has broken all past records. And who knows how many tourists it's affected?"

Slipping his hand into his pocket, D.C. touched the small package his mother had given him earlier in the police station. He'd told her what he wanted, and she'd gotten it for him. As his fingers closed around it, he saw the diamond burn more fiercely. A mix of certainty and fear moved through him. The Rubinov *had* done its work, as far as he was concerned. But he still had to convince Fiona of that.

Suddenly a bit restless, D.C. circled the display case. It was a few minutes short of 5:00 p.m. Chance had gone over the timetable with him when he'd called to let them know he and Natalie were on the way to the hospital. Once the halls were cleared, D.C. was to step out and signal Fiona to bring Amanda in. After she'd had time with the diamond, he'd call in the security from the insurance company and they'd escort Charity Watkins and Regina Meyers into the exhibition room.

But would Amanda remember anything? And if she did, would it be enough?

D.C.'s phone rang. One glance told him it was Jase. "What have you got?"

"The jackpot, thanks to Franks identifying Kate McGowan. Her other alias is Kate Lewen."

"The mother of Kathryn and Charity?"

"Correct. Kate McGowan was the name she used professionally as a jewelry designer. Lewen was her birth name. However, there's no record of either of those names being used for the last ten years."

"She used Kate McGowan with Arthur Franks," D.C. said.

"I don't doubt she did. But she used Dr. Regina Meyers when she went to work with Gregory Shalnokov. And she had a fully documented identity to go with the new name. I believe Kate may be as good at creating new identities as she is at creating copies of legendary jewelry. One of my men is working on that as we speak. One other thing you might find interesting. One of my men interviewed Kate's sister. She claims that Kate Lewen had very little contact with her daughters until ten years ago. But from that time on, she became very involved in each and every decision they made."

D.C. was pocketing his phone when Regina Meyers and Charity Watkins walked into the room. They were early, and he felt the premonition of danger almost as keenly as he'd felt it that night in the sculpture garden.

Meyers reached him first. "I'm Dr. Regina Meyers and I'm here to oversee the transfer of the Rubinov and return it to its owner."

He had a split second to decide how to play it. Taking out his cell phone, he said, "You're a bit early. I'll just contact the security detail."

She drew a gun out of her purse. "No need. They're a bit incapacitated at the moment." She jerked her head in the direction of the guard. "Tell him not to be a hero."

"Don't be a hero, Bobby," D.C. said.

"Charity?" There was a note of impatience in Regina's voice.

Out of the corner of his eye, D.C. saw the blonde director

punch a button on an electronic device and the lights in and around the display case suddenly blinked out. Keeping his gaze steady on Regina, D.C. pressed one number into his phone as he returned it to his pocket.

"Is that how you jammed the security systems and the cameras the other day when you tried to steal it?" D.C. asked.

Regina shrugged. "Why mess with success? It worked. Charity, get the necklace."

The blonde director started to play a small recorder and he heard the lock on the display case click. He had to stall them until Fiona picked up her cell. "Why are you taking this kind of risk? In half an hour, the diamond will be on its way back to your boss."

Something akin to hatred flashed into Regina's eyes. "I can't allow that. Once he gets it back, I may never see it again. And it's mine. I knew it the first time I held it in my hands."

"When was that?" D.C. asked.

"Ten years ago. Shalnokov contacted me because he wanted a copy made. I thought I could steal it then, but he never left me alone with it. He knew how I felt about it, how attached I was, so he offered me a job. I thought that living in the same house with it might be enough. But it's not. It only makes it worse. Knowing it's there and not having it. Not being able to see it, to hold it."

Her voice was growing more shrill as she spoke. "Once Shalnokov gets his hands on it again, he'll bury it in that safe. And I'll be trapped again."

From the look in Regina's eyes, Shalnokov wasn't the only one obsessed with the diamond, D.C. noted. And there was a rapt expression on Charity's face as she opened the display case. D.C. recalled the legend. It wasn't just love that the diamond inspired. It was greed and obsession, also.

"It's unfortunate that your first attempt to steal it was a failure," D.C. said.

"It shouldn't have failed," Regina insisted. "It was ten years in the planning. I should have the diamond right now."

"I certainly did my part," Charity said. "I convinced Shalnokov to bring the necklace to the National Gallery. However, my sister's skills fell short. She had to involve one of her students."

"Charity, we don't have time today for sibling rivalry," Regina said, her voice tight and still a bit shrill.

D.C. kept his voice calm and matter-of-fact. "You're going to fail again. The guards in the security room won't wait as long this time before they come down and check the room."

"They know that the transfer is taking place today. I'm betting they won't expect the same thing twice," Regina said.

D.C. had to grant her that one. He, Chance and Fiona—none of them had foreseen this happening. He recalled what Jase had told him about Kate/Regina's ability to create new identities. No doubt she and her daughters would step into new ones as soon as they left the building.

"Charity…" Regina urged.

"Got it."

Out of the corner of his eye, D.C. saw the blonde lift the necklace out of the case.

His time had just run out.

"WHAT DID YOU DO THEN?" Fiona asked Amanda. Her feeling that something was wrong grew stronger. She shifted her gaze to the door to the exhibition room. It had only been a matter of seconds since Regina and Charity had pushed through it. But the hall had emptied. The security guard should have signaled them to come in.

"I left the café to find Billy. I didn't want to believe what I'd overheard, but I had to warn him." Amanda leaned back and closed her eyes. "It was nearly closing time when I spotted him going through a door marked Employees Only. When I pushed through it, he disappeared through another door, and it was locked. I waited for him. When he came out, he had the Rubinov in his hands. He didn't see me. He was holding the necklace out in front of him, just staring at it. Then everything happened so fast. All I could think of was that if he didn't have the necklace, no one would hurt him—that they'd have to wait until they recovered the diamond. So I grabbed it and ran. I ducked into the first ladies' room I found and I waited there until one of the guards came in to clear it out. Then I got out of the gallery. I'm not even sure where I went. All I could think of was that if I could get to General Eddinger, she would know what to do."

Fiona glanced up at the door. Neither D.C. nor the security guard had poked their heads out.

When her cell rang, she flipped it open. But it was Regina Meyers's voice she heard on the other end. "Why mess with success? It worked the first time. Charity, get the necklace."

Fear formed a spiked fist in her stomach. "Amanda, I'm going to leave you here. Just for a second. I want to make sure they're ready for you."

Then, pulling out her gun, she tore down the hall and very quietly opened the door to the exhibition room. The security guard and D.C. saw her right away, but Charity and Regina had their backs to her. Charity was lifting the Rubinov out of the opened glass case.

"Not even that gun is going to get you out of here," D.C. said.

Even as her stomach sank, Fiona made herself focus on the facts. D.C. wanted her to know that Regina Meyers had a gun. And it was pointed at him.

"Oh, yes, it will," Meyers said. "It has to. All the waiting and planning won't be wasted this time. I've come too far. I might even take you along as hostage, just to be sure."

Fiona slipped out of her shoes and moved farther into the room.

"C'mon, Charity. Our ride's waiting." Regina gestured with the gun to get D.C. moving toward the service door. "After you, Captain."

"Right," Charity grumbled. "She stays where it's safe."

D.C. took a step back. "One more question. Ten years ago, when Shalnokov put the Rubinov out of your reach and found a way to keep you with him—was that when you came up with the idea of involving your daughters? Because you decided they might prove useful in your long-term goal of getting your hands on the necklace?"

"Is that why—" As Charity whirled to face her mother, the necklace slipped through her fingers and clattered to the floor. Regina's gun wavered for the first time.

Fiona raced forward. She saw the flash of D.C.'s cane, heard it connect with Meyers's gun arm an instant before she slammed into the woman's side. They fell to the floor together. The roar of the shot blocked the sound of Fiona's head smacking into the side of the display case.

Stars spun in front of her eyes as she rolled off Regina and grabbed the necklace.

"It's mine! It's mine!" The sounds Regina made were those of a wild animal as she dove for Fiona and the two of them rolled across the floor. Fiona gripped the necklace tight as Regina's hands closed around her throat.

Then suddenly the older woman was plucked off of her. Even as D.C. subdued Regina, she kept screaming. "It's mine! It's mine!"

When Fiona got herself upright, she still had the necklace, and she noted that Bobby had his gun aimed at Charity Watkins. Still, Regina screamed.

Over the din, D.C. said, "I see you got my call, Lieutenant. Good job."

15

D.C. STOOD WITH CHANCE just outside the glass wall of Natalie Gibbs-Mitchell's hospital room. Every inch of space inside the room was occupied by females, laughing and talking. The center of attention, of course, was Chance and Natalie's new daughter, Noelle, who'd arrived just after the stroke of midnight on Christmas Eve.

D.C. couldn't seem to take his eyes off of Fiona, who sat at the foot of the bed holding the baby. She was there, and she was safe. Those final moments in the exhibition room were still vivid in his mind. Fiona's head smacking into the display case, an obsessed woman's hands closing around her throat.

Fiona Gallagher was quite a woman. And she was his. Impatience bubbled up. He was going to have to settle that. Soon.

But there hadn't been time. And now she was in the midst of a crowd. Among the others filling the room to capacity were Natalie's sisters, Rory and Sierra, and best friends, Sophie and Mac. It was when his mom, his sister, General Eddinger and Amanda had arrived that Chance had signaled the men out of the room. Then he'd dispatched his two brothers-in-law to pick up some food and champagne from a local deli.

D.C. was looking forward to both. The past twenty-four hours had been jam-packed, leaving little time for food or thought. Kathryn Lewen had been picked up in a car that had been waiting in a loading zone outside the National Gallery. He and Fiona had escorted all three women into the station where they'd promptly called their lawyers.

"Sorry I couldn't be there at the end," Chance said, joining him at the window.

"You had better things to do." D.C.'s gaze remained steady on Fiona. He slipped his hand into his pocket and gripped the small package that had been burning a hole there. He had a plan, he reminded himself. He just needed time to put it into action.

"What's the status of the case right now? I know that Fiona called Natalie with updates this morning. But that will still be her first question when this crowd leaves. In fact, she's probably grilling Fiona about it right now."

D.C. had to agree. His mother was holding the baby now and Fiona had moved closer to Natalie on the bed.

"You married a cop," D.C. said.

"Yeah. You thinking of doing the same?"

"Yeah." He wasn't just thinking of it. He was going to do it. If he could just get her alone. It had been crowded enough at the station, but here at the hospital, privacy didn't seem to be even remotely available.

"If you need a job close to the D.C. area, I can offer you one. Of course, Natalie's going to offer you one, too."

D.C. shot a look at Chance. "Really?"

Chance nodded. "And she can dangle the possibility of working with a great partner in front of you."

"How did you know that I might be looking for a new job?" Then before Chance could answer, he said, "General Eddinger."

Chance merely smiled. "I'm taking the fifth." He glanced at his watch. "My brothers-in-law should be back shortly with the refreshments. While we wait, why don't you update me on the case?"

"Regina Meyers alias Kate McGowan and Kate Lewen is a bitter and broken woman. But she's smart, and her lawyer is hoping for a deal. He's already hinting at some kind of diminished-capacity defense based on her overpowering obsession with the necklace. Together, they're painting as sympathetic a picture of her as they can. She claims that while her obsession was with the diamond, Shalnokov's obsession was with her. He fell in love with her, and he used the Rubinov to keep her with him for the last ten years."

"A triangle of obsession and greed," Chance murmured.

"Yeah. She was evidently threatening to leave Shalnokov two years ago. That's when he put the necklace up for auction at Christie's, and she thought she'd finally get her hands on it. Afterward, she realized that the only reason he did that was to dangle the possibility in front of her and make her stay. The incident only made her more determined, and by that time, she had her backup plan in place."

"The two daughters," Chance said.

D.C. nodded. "For years, she'd showered them with attention and got them as fascinated with the necklace as she was. She influenced every decision in their lives including career choices. Charity says she married her husband five years ago to secure her position at the National Gallery."

"And the other daughter? The professor?"

D.C. smiled. "She's much less forthcoming. She won't admit to any involvement, and she's distancing herself from her mother and sister. She claims she was waiting outside the National Gallery because the three of them had dinner plans. She also says she had no idea of Billy Franks's involvement in the attempted theft until he came to her house in a panic two days ago."

"And she didn't go to the police because?" Chance asked.

"He was a student of hers. And after all, the necklace hadn't been stolen, had it? But her sister Charity is singing a different tune. Lots of sibling rivalry there. And Billy is filling in a lot of blanks. He tipped us off that it was Kathryn who rented the van he and his friends used. It was also her gun that he used to hit Amanda on the head. He claims Lewen gave it to him just in case he needed it."

"Do you know why they involved Billy Franks?" Chance asked.

"He had the skills to get to the diamond and Kathryn didn't. Billy also says that Kathryn Lewen recruited him to come to the university in the first place. I'm betting that was Regina's idea. After all, she knew of his grandfather's talents and had probably done her research on young Billy. Fiona believes that Billy developed a crush on Kathryn Lewen and she used that to lure him into doing what she wanted."

"Is he going to have to do jail time?" Chance asked.

"At Amanda's request, General Eddinger has hired him a very good lawyer. And I understand that Arthur Franks has invited him for a visit."

"Who decided to eliminate Billy?" Chance asked.

"I'm betting on Regina pulling *all* the strings. She's the one Amanda heard talking about it. If the original plan had worked, all three women would probably have returned to their jobs with no one being the wiser for some time. But Billy would have been a liability. After waiting for ten years, Kate/Regina wouldn't take a chance that anyone would spoil her plan."

"And Amanda spoiled everything," Chance said.

D.C. smiled. "Indeed, she did. And Regina panicked. That's why I think she tried to eliminate Billy and his friends. And, of course, she had to switch to a much riskier backup plan. Once that necklace had left the National Gallery with your security detail, she believed she would never see it again. Her obsession with it took over and she risked everything."

"She just might have pulled it off. That diamond has a lot of power," Chance said.

D.C. fingered the bag in his pocket. "It does."

In the distance, he heard the laughter of Chance's brothers-in-law, but he never took his eyes off of Fiona. When she rose from the bed and turned to meet his gaze through the glass, every other thought slipped from his mind.

FOR A MOMENT FIONA DIDN'T MOVE. She just stood there, her gaze locked on D.C. Once more she felt that pull, as intense and irresistible as it had been from the first time she'd seen him across the display case. She moved toward him. Natalie's room was small, the distance to the door no more than ten feet, but she felt like she was walking the last mile. Nerves danced in her stomach. She and D.C. had to get back to the station. There was still a lot of work to do, and she'd already lingered longer than she should have.

But her nerves had nothing to do with the case and everything to do with D.C. Their work together was drawing to a close. It was Christmas morning, and she'd spent the past ten minutes holding a little Christmas miracle. Noelle Gibbs-Mitchell. D.C.'s mother had once more invited her to join the Campbell family to celebrate Christmas. But they'd switched locations from Manhattan to Baltimore because of the case. She wanted to join them.

Fiona Gallagher, the woman who avoided Christmas like the plague, wanted to spend the holiday with people who were still strangers to her and with a man she was just coming to know.

And that wasn't all she wanted. She wanted D. C. Campbell.

When she stepped into the hall, Chance ushered his food-laden brothers-in-law into the room, shutting the door behind them. For a moment, neither she nor D.C. spoke.

Christmas was a time for wishes, Fiona reminded herself. She'd believed that once. She'd already been granted one wish—the case that would keep her busy during the holidays. Now she was just going to have to take a risk and make another.

"D.C.—"

"Fiona."

They spoke at the same time. Then the silence fell again.

D.C. studied her and tried to find the words. She was the only woman he'd ever met who'd had this power to tie his tongue into knots.

"I want to—" This time they not only spoke at the same time, they said the same words.

D.C. gripped the package in his pocket and cleared his throat. "One of us has to take the lead. And there's something I want to say."

When she nodded, her expression reminded D.C. a bit of a deer trapped in the headlights. Behind him, he heard a cart being pushed down the hall. He could have picked a better place, a better time. Frustration rolled through him. He hadn't been able to pick and choose anything where Fiona was concerned.

"Things between us have happened fast," he said. "So I was thinking maybe you'd like to slow things down, do something…traditional?"

"Traditional? Like what?"

It was more than nerves he saw in her eyes now. Was it panic? Or laughter?

Before his tongue could tie itself up again, he said, "I could give you more romance."

Her brows shot up. "*More* romance? You've already taken me dancing and on a winter picnic. You've cooked a meal for me, and we've had date talk. What else do you have in mind?"

An image filled his mind. And because he wanted nothing more than to grab her and kiss her, D.C. fisted his free hand at his side. "I know you like to see the end of the road before you start down it."

Fiona lifted her chin. "And you like to improvise. Why don't I take the lead?"

He nodded. "Go ahead, Lieutenant."

Fiona swallowed hard and continued to study him. A tall male who'd invaded her whole life. An understanding man who saw things in her that she was just discovering. There was no way to figure out the odds. No way to see the end of the road. All she could rely on was instinct.

And after all, hadn't it been instinct that kept her believing in Amanda Hemmings's innocence? Hadn't it been instinct or something very close that had brought her to the Rubinov exhibit in the first place? No matter the risk, she had to go with instinct now.

Stepping forward, she held out her hand, and D.C. took it in his. "I know that I told you I only wanted something temporary. But I've changed my mind."

When he said nothing, she lifted her chin. "A woman has a right to do that."

"Tell me what you want, Fiona. Spell it out."

She drew in a deep breath. "I want to share your clean slate and help you write on it."

For a moment, a moment she thoroughly enjoyed, he simply stared at her. Then her words hit him, and dropping his cane, he swept her up in his arms and twirled her around. And around.

Her head was still spinning when he set her down and kissed her soundly. From the inside the hospital room came a muffled cheer. Neither of them paid it any heed.

"For once, we're on the same page, Lieutenant." He reached into his pocket, pulled out a small box and flipped it open. "However, I'm going to give you one more chance to opt for something traditional."

Fiona stared at the blue diamond.

Then he dropped to one knee. "I love you, Fiona Gallagher. And I want you to write on that clean slate with me, too. Will you?"

With her throat tightening, Fiona dropped to her knees and met D.C.'s eyes. "I love you, D. C. Campbell. And I will."

From inside the hospital room came another cheer. After one last, long kiss, D.C. said, "By the way, D.C. stands for Duncan Charles."

Fiona grinned at him. "That's your deepest, darkest secret?"

"Pretty much. At Jase's advice I switched to the initials before I entered school. He warned me if I didn't, the other kids would probably nickname me 'Donut.'"

Laughing, Fiona and D.C. rose and turned to watch the crowd gathered in Natalie's room raise their champagne glasses in a toast.

Epilogue

D.C. HANDED FIONA a glass of champagne and leaned close. "Well, what do you think?"

Fiona surveyed the large living room of the Baltimore colonial where D.C.'s family had gathered to celebrate Christmas. Nancy was refilling champagne glasses, and Darcy was trying to cram enormous piles of discarded wrapping paper into a plastic garbage bag.

Fiona's head was still spinning a little, but she thought she had most of the names straight. Jase, who had his mother's coloring, was sitting on the other side of D.C., and his fiancée, Maddie, was perched on the arm of the sofa next to him.

It was easy to keep Cash Landry straight because with his tanned skin and lanky build he made her think of a cowboy. And that was what he was. He owned a ranch next to the one Maddie owned in Santa Fe. Cash's fiancée, Jordan, sat with him on a love seat. Fiona had had some trouble distinguishing identical twins Maddie and Jordan until D.C. had pointed out that Jordan would always be the one wearing killer heels. Fiona could relate to that.

She turned to D.C. "What I think is that you inherited your much touted ability to improvise from your mother."

"You got that right," Jase said. "Only our mother never seems to land herself in the kind of scrapes that D.C. does."

The Campbell family's plans to meet in Manhattan on Christmas Eve had been scrapped once Nancy had decided that Fiona and D.C. were going to be delayed. Then she'd shifted everyone to plan B: meet at the family home in Baltimore on Christmas evening.

"She's amazing," Fiona said. When she and D.C. had arrived a few hours ago, there'd been presents piled under the tree, a bluesy version of "Silver Bells" drifting out of the stereo and the scent of food and candles in the air.

Something tightened in Fiona's throat as she turned to meet her new fiancé's eyes. "She even bought presents for me. When did she have time to do that?"

Jase spoke up. "When D.C. and I were kids, we always thought Mom had a direct line to Santa's toy shop."

"What makes you think I don't?" Nancy asked as she tipped champagne into his glass.

Fiona turned to her. "I don't have anything for anyone."

Nancy set her champagne bottle down, took Fiona's hands and drew her to her feet. "You gave me the best present you could when you agreed to marry D.C. I've been wanting to get him off my hands for a long time."

As the room filled with laughter, Nancy hugged Fiona. "Magic diamond or not, I knew the moment I saw you in the sculpture garden that you were the one for Duncan. Mother's intuition tells me you'll be good for him."

"He'll be good for me," Fiona said.

"Here, here." D.C. raised his glass. "I can drink to that."

When Fiona sat back down, D.C. leaned close and said, "The tradition Mom treasures the most is that we're all together. We've always come together for Christmas if we possibly can. You're a part of us now."

You're a part of us now. Fiona felt a burning sensation

behind her eyes. Blinking, she slipped a hand into D.C.'s. "You said you wanted to give me new memories of Christmas, and you have. Thank you. Next year, I don't think I'll be wishing for a case to get me through to the New Year."

D.C. leaned down to brush his mouth softly over hers. "We're just beginning, Fiona."

"Yes, we are. But I'm not sure you'll ever be able to top this Christmas. This year I got you, my very own Christmas male."

"And I got you. Forever." Leaning down, he covered her mouth with his.

Washington Post—December 26
Private Amanda Hemmings to Be Honored

Police Commissioner James Cavanaugh announced today that Private Amanda Hemmings will receive the key to the city for her heroic actions in preventing the theft of the Rubinov necklace from the National Gallery.

And in the wake of the arrests that have been made, Gregory Shalnokov has announced that he intends to put the legendary Rubinov necklace on permanent loan to the National Gallery.

So true love will continue to abound in our nation's Capital for some time to come!

THE CHARMER &
HER SECRET FLING

(2-IN-1 ANTHOLOGY)

BY KATE HOFFMANN &
SARAH MAYBERRY

The Charmer

Publisher Alex has never had any trouble
attracting the opposite sex, but he was amazed
to be saved from a snowstorm and then
seduced senseless by sexy Tenley.

Her Secret Fling

Star reporter Jake rubs Poppy the wrong way until
they go on a trip together and the relationship goes from
antagonistic to hedonistic. A secret fling seems delicious...

SPONTANEOUS
BY BRENDA JACKSON

Whenever Kim and Duan meet up, the passion between them is
hot, intense...spontaneous. And things really heat up when Duan
accompanies her to a wedding.

SEXY MS. TAKES
BY JO LEIGH

Start the New Year off with a bang with these three sizzling stories in
one Blazing book!

On sale from 17th December 2010
Don't miss out!

*Available at WHSmith, Tesco, ASDA, Eason
and all good bookshops*

www.millsandboon.co.uk

1210/14

With This Fling...
by Kelly Hunter
Charlotte Greenstone's convenient, fictional fiancé *inconveniently* resembles sexy stranger Greyson Tyler! Grey agrees to keep Charlotte's secret as long as they enjoy *all* the benefits of a real couple...

Girls' Guide to Flirting with Danger
by Kimberly Lang
When the media discover that marriage counsellor Megan Lowe is the ex-wife of an infamous divorce attorney, Megan has to take the plunge and face her dangerously sexy ex.

Juggling Briefcase & Baby
by Jessica Hart
A weekend working with his ex, Romy, and her baby, Freya, has corporate genius Lex confused. Opposites they may be, but Lex's attraction to happy-go-lucky Romy seems to have grown stronger with the years...

Deserted Island, Dreamy Ex
by Nicola Marsh
Starring in an island-based TV show sounded blissful, until Kristi discovered her Man Friday was her ex, Jared Malone. Of course, she doesn't feel *anything* for him, but can't help hoping he'll like her new bikini...

On sale from 3rd December 2010
Don't miss out!

Available at WHSmith, Tesco, ASDA, Eason and all good bookshops
www.millsandboon.co.uk

2 FREE BOOKS
AND A SURPRISE GIFT

We would like to take this opportunity to thank you for reading this Mills & Boon® book by offering you the chance to take TWO more specially selected titles from the Blaze® series absolutely FREE! We're also making this offer to introduce you to the benefits of the Mills & Boon® Book Club™—

- **FREE home delivery**
- **FREE gifts and competitions**
- **FREE monthly Newsletter**
- **Exclusive Mills & Boon Book Club offers**
- **Books available before they're in the shops**

Accepting these FREE books and gift places you under no obligation to buy, you may cancel at any time, even after receiving your free books. Simply complete your details below and return the entire page to the address below. You don't even need a stamp!

YES Please send me 2 free Blaze books and a surprise gift. I understand that unless you hear from me, I will receive 3 superb new books every month, including a 2-in-1 book priced at £5.30 and two single books priced at £3.30 each, postage and packing free. I am under no obligation to purchase any books and may cancel my subscription at any time. The free books and gift will be mine to keep in any case.

Ms/Mrs/Miss/Mr_____ Initials _____

Surname _____

Address _____

_____

_____ Postcode _____

E-mail _____

Send this whole page to: Mills & Boon Book Club, Free Book Offer, FREEPOST NAT 10298, Richmond, TW9 1BR